Praise f

"At once religious; both bursting with appetite and laced with self-denial."
— *Pacific Rim Review of Books*

"This moving novel captures the struggle of ordinary, flawed people to find depth and meaning in a postmodern world saturated in superficiality. Cavalli offers his readers affirmation that the sacred resources of literature, art, love, and spirituality can provide a sustenance that is both embodied and transcendent."
— Sharon Alker, Professor of English, specializing in 18th-Century Literature & Romanticism

"A weird beauty"
— *Edinburgh Book Review*

"That documentary and myth are in active tension defines the form and appeal of the novel. I especially liked the documentary dimension, the extended and precise detail — on native flora, engineering, geology, first aid protocols, pop music, sacred music, ballistics, and much more. All this against a story line of transcendent mystery."
— Laurie Ricou, Professor Emeritus of Canadian Literature, University of British Columbia

for Catrina from Vic Cavalli

Vic Cavalli

The Road to Vermilion Lake

Harvard Square Editions
New York
2017

The Road to Vermilion Lake
Copyright © 2017 Vic Cavalli

None of the material contained herein may be reproduced or stored without permission of the author under International and Pan-American Copyright Conventions.

This is a work of fiction. Names, characters, places and incidents either are the products of the author's imagination or are used fictitiously. Any resemblance to actual persons, living or dead, events or locales are entirely coincidental.

ISBN 978-1-941861-40-0
Printed in the United States of America
Published in the United States by
Harvard Square Editions
www.harvardsquareeditions.org

CHAPTER ONE:

I was twenty-one when H & S hired me as a blaster's helper and first-aid attendant. After struggling through three years of college, I needed to work outdoors. I started with my basic ticket and they paid for my annual upgrading until I had an Industrial Class A card in my wallet. No matter how bad some guy was damaged, my job was to keep him alive until the chopper took him. Before we forced the road in, the aerial photos showed a vast turquoise edge pressed by virgin sand and verdant wild fruit blossom and free-fallen granite stones scattered like massive seeds come to rest in the countless crevices of the surrounding mountains.

It took seven years to reach Vermilion Lake. And blasting three hundred million tons of rock out of the Fertilio Mountains, shook the living hell out of the place. Prehistoric cacti pods—dormant for thousands of years—were exploded into the sky and fell back to the earth. Along the road edges, walls of prickly cylinders formed. Cutting those down was hard—a lot of white hand disease and spine wounds. As the job moved on, as far as we could see the terrain was curvaceous and dry and aching with fertility. Wherever underground streams gushed up fresh and clear, and soaked the earth and pooled, they triggered succulent growth. Pale golden leaves of spiraled sand formed. Purple water weeds pushed down roots near the edges. Bottomless shafts of bubbling clear light, deep and cold, sprang up through the sharp-edged black granite shards in the sandy shade.

Joe Bahsta—with his fierce head of curly silver hair and cold gray eyes—was our head blaster. And as he slid dynamite sticks into the long thin holes we'd drilled into the rock, one at a time, delicately nudging them down to seat in the base of each hole and then stacking them next to a vein fuse line, old Vince Alto would always cry out to him from his foreman's distance, "Be as careful as hell with those sticks, Joe. Don't blow us all to kingdom come!" Then Vince would move into a crouch like an arthritic cougar, and he would silently wait with the rest of us huddled behind iant boulders and Ponderosa pine cover as we squatted on beds of needles. With our bulky aircraft mechanics ear protectors on, we prepared for the sudden boom and the granite shower.

I always thought of Sally Nostal just before the charges blew: her beautiful blue eyes, her long gently curled black hair, her snug powder blue cashmere V-neck sweater cut to the perfect depth. Over her flawless white skin descended a thin fine gold chain taut with some mysterious weight hidden between her fragrant breasts. She was all subtle fragrance and mystery to me. She was the first woman I had ever seriously kissed.

One Friday night after searching for any unlocked car we could find in a dimly lit alley off Victoria Drive in Vancouver, with the warm June rain gushing down, we found a hot 1965 Shelby Mustang some guy hadn't locked. I said "Ladies first," as she flexed in with her killer tight jeans, and then following her with millions of years of instinct, I slipped in through the rain-beaded metallic blue passenger door and closed it with a quiet firm pull as water started to fleck the upholstery. Sally gave me a wide smile and, snuggling closer, whispered in my ear, "If this was my car, all I'd want to do is ride around in it all day." I don't know what brand of gum she was chewing, but I'll never forget how fresh and sweet her mouth tasted and those pretty teeth and lips.... BOOM! And her soft chest against mine, and the scent of her skin.... BOOM!

Before every blast, as we worked our way to Vermilion Lake, I thought of her perfect mouth, her beautiful V-neck with that chain descending, the two of us in perfect health immersed in the warm nucleus of that soaked night in Vancouver in that unlocked Shelby and the sound of the rain on its sheet metal roof and the distant street lights glowing and sparkling bus wires and a few signs lighting the interior where the smell and taste of that gum and her lips and her clean white teeth gave me both barrels and blew my mind for life. It was a good memory to detonate twice a day for seven years. And every night of those seven years, there alone in my tent on the edge of camp—after reading some lines from Keats, Whitman, or Rilke—as I shut my eyes to sleep, I thought of Sally and wondered if she ever thought of me. I could see her, and then everything dissolved.

I treated countless construction-related wounds during those seven years, and also several grizzly bear injuries: near-severed limbs dangling from tendons, skulls scratched to the bone, and one ear and cheek bitten off as if ripped by a large-tooth two-man fallers saw. As I bandaged up these poor mangled bastards, before they were flown out to the hospital, I reminded them that in the old pioneer days the best looking women were turned on by grizzly bear wounds. I didn't really know if it was true, but often around the night fires after a long day's work and several beer, the older blasters claimed it was certain. They swore, virtually in unison, that in their distant youths they had seen knockouts who were crazy about brutalized remnants of men.

The big bears only wandered into camp in the spring. They were starved and fearless and took whatever food they wanted. Some even ignored the rifle fire as they were being shot at and kept eating and burying their massive heads in our storage containers of fish and meat. I only killed one bear with Lee's .375 H&H, and that was in self-defense and because Vince was away getting supplies. Of the nine bears killed while I was on the job, eight were shot by Vince with his .378 Weatherby. More common wounds were massive gashes from flying granite shards, and a steady stream of minor eye injuries. In seven years, no one was blinded. That stands out in my memory. Those were hard but good years spent close to the land, good except for the tragedy during our last month of work. The story I got from my buddy Dave Abbracci was that the emergency scene and dental records showed that a young woman alone in a metallic green Bronco was off-roading right up in back of us when the rock face blew. He said, "Her vehicle was covered in massive stones, and once they dug her out and cut open her flattened Bronco with the Jaws of Life what was left of her was unrecognizable. She was gone." That accident was the only irreversible sorrow during our project. All we could do was keep working until we were done. My last blast was on my twenty-eighth birthday, and as always, Sally's beautiful mouth was there as the explosion echoed. She was there, and then she faded.

Now that the road was in, the construction of Vermilion Lake Village began. At least 90 percent of the road crew moved on to other road projects in British Columbia. There were a lot of healed men suddenly blown widely into the province like OO buckshot loads out of a 12 gauge short-barrel security gun, but I decided to stay on and work first-aid construction.

Espero Developers had a unique vision for the village. They believed the lake was too beautiful to be randomly approached, and the Swiss-based architectural firm wanted to use the terrain as an experiment, a utopian pilot project. The lakefront was a clear edge pressed by pure sand, the powder left behind by ancient glaciers. Mute swans nested all along the lake's shoreline, and perpetually, white-headed eagles muscularly swirled high above and reflected themselves into the lake's yielding surface. From the air the lake was the shape of a heart carved into an alder tree in a campsite area where youth drink heavily. The subdivision plans for the lake showed a northwest park section where Windhover Creek entered the lake's center, and a southeast village core section where Windhover Creek exited its center, each segment of land ninety square miles in area. This plan pictured the icy current of melted snow descending from the surrounding mountains as a diagonal arrow through the lake, resembling a heart with an arrow through it carved on a tree with the lovers' initials in the center. Any couples living on the shores of Vermilion Lake, or swimming in its waters, or drifting in small non-motorized boats, would be in the romantic equivalent of the Bermuda Triangle.

I learned from one of our surveyors that the concept was the brainchild of an environmental architect from New York. On the company's website no photo was given and her name was listed simply as Ms. J. Nostal. That caught my attention. I filled out the contact form and sent her what was probably the longest online inquiry she'd ever received. I took a chance by explaining who I was, my first-aid construction position with Espero Developers, and my admiration for her utopian geographical development experiment at Vermilion Lake. I threw in some poetic observations about the beauty of her vision, and I attached a photo explaining that I wanted her to know who she was writing to, as she must get countless inquiries from strangers. Then I signed the message formally with, Sincerely, Thomas Neal Tems. For all I knew she was a fifty-year-old married career woman, and so obviously I went easy with the poetry.

Three days later she answered my message with a surprisingly long energetic message of her own. She was only twenty-five and a recent graduate of Notre Dame's School of Environmental Design. She was blown away that her first major project was being received so well and was actually being implemented. I was caught off guard by her explanation of Hemingway's comment about Fitzgerald's unconscious early writing style as similar to the dust on a brightly colored butterfly's wing. She said, "The delicate transiency of that image pervades my concept of home and true love." I felt a bit out of my league, but I was intrigued. She didn't mention anything about a partner or being married or children and said she would be on site at the lake in three weeks. She owned one of the best lakefront lots, and she was planning to build soon. She urged me to not refer to her as Ms.

Nostal, but rather just to call her Johnny. That got my attention too.

Will New, the head of our surveying unit, a thin man in his early forties with a thick head of black hair combed straight back (which gave him a kind of seriously into classical music look), needed to work with her in person as he was running into geological issues with the patterning of roads as she'd schematized them. She said she'd be staying at the local Gold Motel during her four day visit and that she was happy to learn that the annual B.C. Classic Car Show would be in town and running from noon to 8:00 p.m. on the days she was visiting. Perhaps she could meet me at the show after work one of those days?

I messaged her back, "Absolutely, I love hot cars. See you then. Tom."

Johnny gave me her cell number and said she'd call me when she got to town. That call would be the first time I heard her voice.

Work was great. I was in good health, not to be proud but simply honest, I was decent looking—185 pounds, 5' 10", 32" waist, bench pressing 225 pounds, dead lifting 365 pounds, running 5 miles a day—dark brown eyes, longish curly black hair, relatively handsome face with a bit of stubble, looking great in faded jeans and a worn Levi shirt, age 28, had a bit of money saved, had dated, had some fun, but as the old U2 chorus goes, "I still [hadn't] found what I [was] looking for," and I reminded myself aloud: "Watch it with the explosive romantic fantasies, man. Just because Sally's lips exploded with each boom of the road into here, doesn't mean some new blast is going to blow your heart to bits here at the lake. She's probably bolted to her career and some handsome architect or painter in the city—bolted with five-inch thick, four-feet long, double-nutted with two massive lock washers, tempered steel bolts, bridge-span grade, each holding five thousand tons of stress, hurricane shear proof, etc., etc.," and I caught myself. "No build up, man. Just meet a smart young woman with interesting ideas and go with the flow. Don't expect anything more than hopefully a friendly meeting with an intelligent person. Don't expect any shaft to be drilled into your chest and dynamite sticks slid in. Don't even think about what her eyes or lips or whatever might look like. Just meet a gifted young woman and then get on with your life."

Eventually, I tried to search the Internet for "Johnny Nostal" images, but she didn't seem to exist, and over the next three weeks I tried to avoid visualizing her, but she took on every bodily form conceivable—from very short to very tall from very thin to very thick and back to thin again, and I decided just to forget her and respond to the date on my calendar the way I'd respond to a blood test appointment: just go there and get it done. And every night as I fell asleep I thought back to Sally in the Mustang in Vancouver, and I wondered if she ever thought of me. Like a Neruda sonnet translated into the physical world, the night sky above Vermilion Lake was always a huge flat-black chrome spaghetti strainer drilled with millions of burning white needle holes. Were Sally's eyes seeing those stars? Was she thinking of me every night as she closed her eyes in sleep? Or was she fading into a luminous dying mist?

During a meeting break at 10:00 a.m. on the first day of the car show, Johnny messaged me that she'd be there at 7:00 p.m. "I'll call you Tom, then meet you in the crowd," she wrote.

After work I went for a jog; then I triple-shaved, showered with Axe soap and shampoo, and splashed on some Brut. I pulled on my best faded jeans and decided to go with a white Levi shirt. I looked as good as possible and got down there. Along the edge of the lake the main drag was lit up with futuristic neon swirls and all traffic was closed off for four blocks in the heart of town. That night there was nothing but sparkling hot cars of every color, and swirling clusters of nostalgic car lovers melting and flowing through Milagro Street. Above us the sky was soft purple and cool and fresh as the sun was setting and millions of distant stars began to emerge. My teen years flashed as I saw mint Dodge Chargers, Thunderbirds, Challengers, Cougars, Camaros, Firebirds, and trucks—especially a brutal metallic-sapphire 54 Ford pickup with a chopped cab, polished oak box flooring, Thrush mufflers, low-rider chassis, and cheater slicks with mags.

Then my cell rang, and as I answered I saw it was Johnny's number. She said she was sitting in a powder blue Shelby near the corner of Milagro and Second Street, "Come and join me, Tom. This car is incredible."

"I'm on my way now."

As I navigated through the thick crowd, my heart throbbed. Then I saw the Shelby next to a stainless steel street light. Its spotlight glare was radiating from the metallic paint and creating a nimbus-like roseate barrier around the vehicle. The crowds flowed around it at a distance like churning winter river water surrounds boulders in steelhead habitat. I could see a woman in the driver's seat of the car, and I entered the circle of light and leaned in through the passenger window and saw her. Her stark green eyes, her long gently curled red hair, her snug peach-colored V-neck sweater cut to the perfect depth. I opened the door and got in.

Over her flawless white skin descended a thin fine gold chain taut with some mysterious weight hidden between her fragrant breasts. She gently reached for the chain and lifted the gold medallion into view. It was indescribably beautiful. She smiled and said, "My sister loves you."

Her form turned to me in the pink envelope of warm light glowing into the Shelby's interior, and she smiled—with perfect white teeth in a perfect fresh mouth, a genetic miracle and mirror of her sister Sally's mouth. But there was an ethereal aching in her eyes. Her lips faintly trembled as she shifted her frame towards me and said, "Sally and I shared everything. Every night, when we lived together in dorm at college, she would snuggle into her layers of pink blankets—with scattered stuffies, their eyes glowing around her—and she'd see herself in your arms under the desert stars, warm, secure, desired—surrounded by looming cacti shadows. She was afraid of what you meant to her. And she didn't know if you ever thought of her."

As she spoke the veil of light permeating our interior slowly withdrew and dimmed and the hundreds crowding the barricaded main street lined with immaculate cars started to hum and rustle and crowd towards us. I looked at her pretty, tear-stained face and suggested we get out of the Mustang and find somewhere else to talk. She stared at me for a moment, then suddenly thrust her hand deep into the left pocket of my Levi shirt and pulled hard as if to tear it, then gently bit her lip seeing my surprise, and said, "All right."

"Let me get your door," I said. Then I got out and felt the crowd push up to the car as I worked my way around the Shelby to let her out.

The sky was now a delicate pink with gentle swirls of blue licking upwards from the sharp stone edges of the mountains surrounding Vermilion Lake. Bright neon bathed the cars and the crowd as she took my hand and held it fast and looked into my eyes as I helped lift her into the windy glow, and I closed the

Mustang's door behind her. She released my hand slowly and smiled and said, "It was good to finally meet you, Tom." I almost let myself tuck a few loose strands of her red hair, like wisps of fire, behind her ear, and for an instant I imagined the taste of her mouth, but everything suddenly felt outrageously public, televised, or recorded, or something, and I pulled back.

CHAPTER TWO:

"Does it seem strange to you that my name is Johnny?" she asked as we worked our way through the crowd. The neon signs flashed thin vein-like colors across us as we floated towards the open lakeside path in the distance down and ahead of us.

"Different, not strange. Why did your parents give you that name?"

"My father was a huge Motown fan, plus a Ford fanatic. He worked as a mechanic for Ford, and apparently he had almost legendary status in the shop."

Her eyes lit up with pride as she talked of her dad.

"He could fix, customize, weld, anything. At work they gave him a private stall in the corner of the shop where he could fix up any car he had bought. He even built a funny car out of a vintage Mustang."

As we broke free of the crowd and wandered towards the shore, we heard car hoods and doors clicking and thumping shut behind us. The noises and lights faded gradually as the sound of wind patterns over the lake grew in volume.

"When the car was finished and the silver paint job was completed, they pushed it out of the Ford shop into the corner of the dealership to fire it up. They knew the noise would be deafening in the shop."

I gestured to Johnny to sit on a bench close to the shore. And we sat there together.

"On the sides of the Mustang in large metallic green lettering were the words *Roman's Chariot*. Roman was his name. When that massive V-8 hemi started, the flames shot six feet out of the headers and its glorious roar was deafening."

I smiled and thought to myself, How many educated women even know what headers are, let alone relish in flames blasting out of them?

She sensed a balloon above my head and asked, "What?"

And I lied and said, "Nothing. Please go on."

"From blocks all around adults and kids ran towards the noise to see what was happening. It was so cool. Mom had brought us sisters down to see the fire up and we were so proud of Dad."

"So Mustangs were his thing?"

"Absolutely," she said and smiled. "Mustangs and deer hunting."

"Deer hunting?"

"Yeah. Being silent in the woods was a mystical thing for Dad, the flipside of headers at the quarter-mile track. He had a book he used to read to us girls. It was called *Bloodties: Nature, Culture, and the Hunt*, by Ted Kerasote. He'd read us a paragraph or two and then pause deep in thought and ask us, "What do you girls make of that?" And we'd try to respond. It was simple but deep. When we were fourteen and twelve he took us girls hunting for mule deer high up on Paleface Mountain, next to Chilliwack Lake in southern B.C. We camped for four days up there. It was strikingly beautiful and rugged, but it wasn't really for me. I was glad to get home. But Sally loved it. She wanted to stay longer. She even asked Dad if he could build a cabin so we could live up there on the mountain. Sally went deer hunting with Dad every fall after that. She learned about guns and knives too and even how to field dress a buck."

"Sally cut open a deer in the bush?"

"I remember, Sally once came home with her hunting clothes soaked in deer blood, and Dad was very proud of her, said she was 'a real pioneer woman.' Mom was against hunting until she tasted that first venison roast. Then she approved of it. She said that the deer's flesh was 'like a sacrament of the wilderness,' and that she could feel all of the fresh mountain air and wild plants that buck had consumed throughout his life, in her, after eating his flesh.

"Sally never talked to you about hunting?"

"Absolutely not, I never would have guessed it. I only knew the soft romantic side of her. I can't even imagine her gutting a deer. Wow. I'm trying to visualize her with her hair up in a camouflage toque, wearing full camo, hunting boots on, nails trimmed and no jewelry."

"You guys didn't have much time together. She would have discussed hunting eventually."

"Did your mom start hunting too?"

"No, her passion was winter steelhead fishing, trying to catch 'chrome bullets.' She grew up near the Skeena Region and her dad used to take her to the Babine River. As a girl she loved fishing and became very good at it. She developed an incredible patience and knowledge of the water. The first time she took me I loved it too, so throughout my teen years Mom and I would go steelhead fishing while Dad and Sally would go hunting. Sally was always the hunter, and I was always the fisher."

"But when you sisters were just kids, Mustangs were top priority for your dad, right?"

"Yeah. When we were small, Dad would come home from work greasy and exhausted. He'd wash up with the bathroom door open, the sink full of frothy soap, and he'd lather his face, neck, and arms to the elbows. Then he'd rinse off with rushing cold water and say 'Ahh! Ahhh! Ahhhh!' as he splashed clean. Then he'd towel dry and head over to the stereo and pop on his old Motown records and kick back with an ice cold Coke. 99.9 percent of the time his first selection would be Wilson Pickett's 'Mustang Sally.' The other 0.1 percent of the time it would be Buddy Guy's cover of that song featuring Jeff Beck."

"So that's the ignition key?" I said and grinned.

"Yeah, Dad was obsessed with that song, crazy about it. It always gave him a jolt after work. So he and Mom agreed that their first daughter had to be named Sally, that was a given."

"And where did Johnny come from?" I asked.

"Dad's passion for funny cars. When we were kids, John Force was the king of the funny car circuit. Dad absolutely idolized him. So when I came along, he convinced Mom to name me Johnny in his honor."

"Okay," I said.

"It's a rare name, and I've actually always liked it. Did you know that since 1881, there have only been 169 girls named Johnny in the United States? And as far as I know, I'm number 169," she said with a smile.

"I certainly did not know that fact," I said as I tilted my head slightly and pressed my lips together to indicate my acceptance of her quirky explanation. "Your dad sounds like an interesting man. I'd love to meet him someday."

Johnny's face became serious and she flinched and it was obvious he was dead.

"My mom Clara, you'll be able to meet someday, she lives in South Bend, but not my dad."

She slid over next to me on the bench and put her arm through mine for support and said, "The last two years of Dad's life were amazing. He was invited to join Vic Potens' FINISH LINE Top Fuel Funny Car racing team and he was happy beyond belief, but then he died in a freak accident in the track area when an 8,700 horsepower motor he was revving exploded. He had just removed the ballistic blankets to check the torque on the supercharger bolts when it blew."

"I'm sorry."

She held my arm tighter and with a few tears blossoming said, "I can't think of a better way for Dad to leave this world than in a roaring explosion of engine parts, smoke and flames. He loved the excitement and danger of racing."

She nervously tried to smile while taking a sighing breath and said, "The Lord gently shifted him into heaven."

"Was your dad religious?"

"Yeah, he was Catholic."

"I don't know much about Catholicism."

"The explanation we grew up with was pretty simple really: God is love, marriage is a big deal, lots of saints and angels, angels everywhere."

Her words were freshening now. And the slightly defiant turned up edge of her upper lip was knocking me out.

"Dad's big dream for us girls was that someday we could go to The University of Notre Dame. But on a mechanic's salary that was pure fantasy. The life insurance we received from the Vic Potens team made that dream possible."

"God works in mysterious ways," she said, simultaneously flinching both at the cliché and the sincere aching whisper in her heart, and then pulled my arm tighter against her.

As we sat there on our bench, Johnny asked me about my family. "Tell me about your family, Tom."

"My past is a bit grim. You won't be encouraged by it."

But she was curious and insisted, and so I explained: "I was the older of two brothers and both my father Jack and younger brother Nick died when I was young."

Johnny held my hand firmly.

"I saw Nick fall dead during a hockey game when he was nine. He was a goalie. The doctors never could determine what caused it. On his death certificate they officially described it as 'an unforeseeable heart attack.' It was as if a colossal invisible puck simply dropped out of the rafters of the ice rink and flattened him."

"What a tragedy," Johnny whispered as she gripped my hand.

"I loved Nick, and his death shook my confidence in life. Yeah, shook my confidence." Johnny looked into my eyes and pressed her lips into a serious rigidity.

I went on, "My mother, Catherine, died from liver failure while I was working on the road crew a few years ago. And my cousins and other relatives are all back east. I'm the lone timber wolf out here in B.C."

"You're not a lone wolf now, Tom," she said and smiled. "Tell me about your dad. Was he a character like my dad?"

"Apparently he was a character, but not like your dad, and I only have my mother's word on that. I never knew him. It's a dark gap in my childhood, probably best forgotten."

"If you're willing, Tom, I'd like to know what happened."

I agreed to tell Johnny as best as I could recall the version I got from Mom, but warned her that Mom was an alcoholic and her credibility was tenuous at best, and that it was a long time ago.

"When I was three years old and Nick was just a baby, Dad was killed by a polar bear in the Inuvik region of The Northwest Territories. He wanted 'to go out in a blaze of fur and blood,' she told me when I was twelve, because he didn't want to live anymore. I guess his mind was a tornado and he couldn't think about how Nick and I might feel being left behind with an alcoholic and her twin sister in Vancouver."

Johnny seemed surprised by the word twin and interjected, "Your mother had a twin sister?"

"Yeah. Identical."

"Is your aunt still living?"

"I think she's still alive in Toronto. I haven't heard from her since Mom's funeral."

Johnny gestured that I should continue.

"I remember sitting at our white, swirled veneer kitchen table, the fly tape hanging like an impotent noose over the sticky counter, the bare hot-white bulb swaying slightly on a chain cord above us, the vehicles below us on Plier Avenue growling by in clusters through the snow—leaving cylinders of silence—and my drunk mother explaining.

"She began something like this: Thomas, you're old enough to know now why you don't have a father. I'm going to tell you this morning. She said, On December 15, in 1987, I had just got home from the Bob Seger concert, I had just paid the sitter, and I was tucking you into bed when out of nowhere your father started pounding on the door. He'd shown up hammered again and I knew he'd keep banging until I let him in. You were only three and you were frightened by the pounding noise. Nick was just a baby, and he was sleeping deeply.

"She took a sip of her White Lady as the ice in her glass metallically tinkled, and continued.

"I cut down the long hallway, unchained the door, and your father burst in and forward—mumbling about someone's heart. He stank of vomit and insisted on seeing you. His full arms, shoulders and back to the waist were covered with a half-executed mural tattoo. Parts of the mural were finished, but the detail feathered off into shaky draft lines smeared with dried surface ink and freshly crusted blood. It seemed as if he had committed himself to a full-torso high-art mural, but then suddenly tore himself away from the artists before they could complete their work. Or maybe someone burst into the parlor and murdered them as they were working, and maybe they had allowed your father to escape, a kind of business card for their sincerity as killers.

"She sniffed at her glass, licked the brim, and paused, waiting for my response, but at age twelve how could I interpret my dead father's new tattoos?"

Johnny listened attentively. A cool wind from the lake was brushing our faces now, her beautiful hair wafted in the mountain air, and she nodded that I should continue.

"Mom went on something to this effect: I could visualize your father staggering in his own vomit in the complete blackness and snow behind the tattoo parlor, gun shots cracking within, and broken glass and broken teeth and stepped-on eyeglasses and the sketched outlines of ghosts scattered like garbage in the puke trails. But your father had no idea where the drawings had come from. The best I could make of his slurred babblings was that when he woke up in his skid row hotel room, his one good eye sticky and opening slowly to the brown stained ceiling, and the moans of a lost man on the floor in the hall outside his door, and the talk of a few sucking on the glass near the bottom of Vancouver's aquarium, and the erratic loud prayers of his teenage neighbor, he felt mugged and raw. At first it seemed like another waking nightmare to him. Carved into his left shoulder was an intricate pattern of black swirls and what seemed to be a cross-like golden tree with an unfinished glob of red blurring energy surrounding it. His right shoulder was similar, but there was a gap of skin like an empty frame waiting for a portrait at the core of the tapestry of lines. What he could see of his back looked like veins of fire flaring and winding upwards from his waist.

"Mom seemed to hesitate as she thought about the flames. Out front, cars and an occasional delivery truck ground through the snow. She pulled her dry long blonde hair behind each ear and walked over to our rattling fridge and took out what was left of the White Lady pitcher and topped up her breakfast glass.

"Your father began yelling and violently hacking phlegm. 'He's only three,' I tried to calm him. 'Don't destroy any hope of innocence in Tom. Sleep it off and see him once you're cleaned up and you've covered yourself. Please. And don't wake up Nick. He's just a baby, for Christ's sake.'

"But he seemed to be deaf, and he pushed towards the couch and collapsed there with gas whistling from the ass of his dirty jeans. He laughed like an insane idiot for a few seconds and then became deathly serious and then fell asleep instantly.

"Then I returned to you and said, 'Daddy will be fine. He loves you sweetheart.' I pulled the door shut and tried to read to you in a comforting voice: 'Long ago, many white bears wandered in the cold mountains of this land.'

"I remember her saying to me: 'Do you remember, Tom?'

"And I remember shaking my head and saying, 'No.'

"Then there was a crash against your wall and your father howled and then strangely became silent—as if his tongue had suddenly been slashed at its root. A few objects tinkled and rolled to their rest. There was a gurgle and then silence again. I continued reading: 'In those days ... '

"As you faded away, I closed the book and placed it beneath your Care Bear lamp. I heard the vehicles struggling for traction in the street below your window, and I walked over and locked it so that neither you nor I could fall out if we were walking in our sleep. Your father's dead weight was against your door as I tried to open it. He had been trying to press his face against the door so as to be closer to us, but had passed out and was lying there on the white rug stinking in a huge pool of his own piss. It wasn't easy, but I pushed the door open and then lugged him into the hall and phoned the manager and told him there was a drunk stranger outside our door."

Johnny interrupted me, "My God, Tom, I'm so sorry you went through that."

"My childhood was not ideal. I think that's enough of my past, Johnny."

But she looked me in the eyes and held my hand firmly and said, "I'm so grateful you've come through all of those trials unscathed, Tom. You've survived."

"Survived, yes, unscathed, that's a different matter."

"If you can continue, Tom, my heart is listening," she said.

"You want the whole slab of granite at once?" I said, wincing a smile.

"Sure. Blast the rock loose and let it fall," Johnny replied in a gruffly rasped construction foreman's tone, and then gave me a sympathetic smile and flashed her green eyes of reassurance.

"Fire in the hole," I grinned back and continued.

"My mother explained that based on the police reports and insurance inquiries after Dad died, this is what must have happened: After your father was released from the Vancouver drunk tank on Main and Hastings, it seems that he immediately cleaned the last scraps of cash out of his bank accounts, pawned his few remaining possessions, and without a driver's license started driving north to Whitehorse in his uninsured, rusted-out pickup truck. All he took was his .22, a knife, an old eiderdown sleeping bag, and a cooler for beer.

"She said that in The Frozen Moose Bar in Williams Lake he got drunk and told one of the bartenders what had happened to his eye. He explained that in 1968 The Yardbirds played at The Gardens Auditorium in Vancouver, and that while shredding at the front edge of the stage, Jimmy Page broke a string during "I'm a Man" and a fragment of the hot wire had shot towards him and pierced his eyeball. He said he was hammered at the concert and didn't seek treatment for over twenty-four hours. Within three weeks his eye burst with puss and he was blind in one eye. He explained how he started to drink heavily, mostly beer and screwdrivers, sitting alone at the center of his massive quadraphonic sound system blasting Who and Stones albums. He ended up in the local B.C. penitentiary by the Fraser River in New Westminster. Your father stopped the story there, but the bartender asked: And then…? So he explained how he met me (during visiting hours at the prison)—a friend's friend—and how we wrote for seven years, and how his poems had floored me. Actually, they did. Your father could write when he was in jail. And he described how when he got out we lived on Plier Avenue (just two blocks from where we are now) and we had two kids together, you and Nick. Your father wouldn't say any more. He just wanted to suck back a few more beers in peace and leave—so the bartender left him alone."

Johnny was attentive and silent, so I continued.

"Mom then told me something along these lines: As far as I understand, in Whitehorse your father got directions and drove until the gravel road ended. He rented a snowmobile from the last Husky gas station on Highway #37 and drove north until he found polar bear tracks. He followed the tracks until a huge bear and her lone cub were in sight. Then he stopped the machine and hunted them on foot. The massive female turned on him right away, but he kept walking towards her, firing his .22 as he crunched forward in the snow. The female came faster as he shot—little blood specks sprouted like flowers on the sow's white shoulders. She crushed him and bit his head like a large nut. Then she and her cub ate most of him. Eventually a priest in Whitehorse recognized his name in the local paper and said a Mass for him. And I kept waiting for him to return, waiting for the pounding at night, until I learned he was dead.

"I clearly remember Mom's exact words, 'That's all I can really tell you about your father, Tom.'

"And I remember what I then asked her, 'Mom, did you ever love Dad?'

"I observed her looking down into the labyrinthine swirls of the white veneer table her White Lady was resting on. She breathed as if a memory was pulling her into the tangled pattern. Then she calmed and looked into my eyes and said (I remember this vividly), 'No. I'm sorry, Tom. I never really loved your father.' I could hear a few swollen flies buzzing behind us on the fly strip over the cutting board—glued there in shock."

I had shared much of Mom's story while looking out at the lake, but now that I had finished, I looked at Johnny and her eyes were filled with tears.

"I'm so sorry you went through that, Tom."

"I don't even know if that story is true, probably it isn't. But that's what I remember Mom telling me and it's all I know about my dad, that and the certainty that he was not there for me and Nick."

Johnny smiled and looked deeply into my eyes and pulled close to me and confidently said, "You will be a miraculously good husband and father, Tom," and then she kissed me very gently on the cheek. Her kiss was kind and gave me hope, and her face against mine left traces of her pure tears on my face. It felt like the weight of that massive slab of granite had been lifted from my shoulders and tossed aside. I was really, deeply glad that I had confided in her.

The sky was now black and starless as clouds had blown in and blanketed the lake. In the distance, reddish-orange fires sprinkled along the shore sparkled. We sat in silence looking over the dark tremulous water. I was absorbing her presence. And I felt the pulse of her heart as she held my arm against her. She smelled incredibly good, and the dark night air was fresh and cool.

After several minutes, Johnny looked at me and said, "I'm so grateful that we met tonight, Tom. You have a deep soul." She looked at me sincerely for a few moments as if she had discovered something. Then she said, "I've got to meet with Will New and the others in the morning. I should get back to the motel and get some rest."

"Absolutely. Let's get you to bed," I said.

As we turned our backs to the lake and headed back towards town, the sound of the wind became increasingly distant and then was replaced by the humming of lights and occasional cars and one logging truck gearing down on the highway in the distance. Johnny's motel was brightly lit with yellow neon everywhere, but very quiet. Lots of parked cars and sleeping travelers. I was so happy to have met her that I didn't want to blow it by saying or doing anything stupid as we separated, so standing there bathed in that yellow glow I just said, "I'm happy that we met tonight, Johnny." She smiled and said, "Me too." Then she gave me a brief hug and dissolved into her room and her door lock clicked and inside a small light came on and looked like an ember.

As I left behind the yellow glow of Johnny's motel, I thought to myself, I am strong. But as I walked home alone down the under-construction patterned streets lined with homes at different stages of framing, in the stretched rays of the street lights they seemed to be the skeletons of lives about to rise from the dead with the hope of moving into the utopian landscape on the developers' horizon, and I thought that my horizon was to finish the job and within a couple of years decide where to drift to next.

On the south side of the lake, at the furthest fringe of the development, were the small prefabricated trailers brought in for Espero's construction crews, and my trailer was #59. It had been my place for the three months I'd worked so far. Like the other trailers it was furnished with cheap basics, a bed, a couch, a table, three chairs. As a place to crash for a single guy working a temporary construction job it was fine, but after meeting Johnny I realized how rootless, probably even pathetic, my world would look to her. That night as I lay in bed staring at the ceiling's fading off-white paint, I could faintly hear a delicate hissing sound. It was the sound of my macho confidence escaping through a microscopic crack. And I wondered what Johnny was thinking as she lay in bed, or if she was already asleep and perhaps dreaming?

As I started to drift off, I visualized fragmented scenes from an old black and white movie I saw on TV as a boy. I can't remember the name of the film, but it was a rich woman / poor man plot where this handsome young broke guy from an ultra-low income apartment building just happens to meet this red-hot high-class woman who sees him from her second floor luxury apartment balcony on the other side of some mediterranean town and they start talking one day. Predictably, this becomes a daily ritual, sparks ignite, it looks like true love, she'd give up everything to be with him, but she has no idea what actually living in his reality would mean. The story reaches a climax as the guy finally realizes the obvious, that the economic gap between them is too great, and he tells her he won't be visiting her anymore. The guy is genuinely unhappy, trying to do the right thing, and his visits do stop. The woman then goes into a severe romantic withdrawal, somehow gets the poor guy's address, and determines to hunt him down and prove her true love. She honestly believes that poverty cannot crush the epic true love they share.

The film's carefully crafted black and white scenes moved in and out of my mind as sleep pressed against me, and the last scene I remembered before finally crashing was her walking up the stairs in his dilapidated building, looking for his floor and then his room number, but as she ascends she's overwhelmed by the sounds of children crying and the violent shouting of husbands and wives raging from behind the thin walls of their cheap apartments, and her nerves are starting to fail. She has never seen anything like this. And then cut.

Then my mind shifted to my first-aid station and I said aloud to myself, "Remember to check Dave's bandage tomorrow. Don't let his hand get infected." A few seconds of black and then I was gone.

CHAPTER THREE:

My work alarm went off at 6:00 a.m., and as always I hit the snooze button. But before the nine minutes were up, and it went off again, a text came in. My phone was vibrating on the windowsill. The early sun was cutting into the trailer windows at 45 degree angles as I jumped up and read the text: "Tom, I really think we need to talk. Can you meet me at our bench tonight at sunset, around nine?" "Our bench," I said aloud to myself, and wrote back, "Absolutely."

With Espero Developers' two hundred plus employees—machine operators and tradesmen of every sort—my first-aid station was usually busy, and that day was typical. Four guys came in over the day with eye injuries, all with the same sharp splinters of plywood blasted into their eyes when using circular saws without safety goggles. I've seen these injuries repeated for years, and I've never understood the macho take on safety glasses. After I got my first eye splinter, I instinctually started wearing them, and I couldn't imagine cutting without them from then on.

The worst were leg injuries. One older guy cut into his thigh with a circular saw, and another young guy wasn't wearing steel-toed boots while clearing brush with a Sandvik and buried the razor-sharp blade between his big and next toe all the way up to the arch. The poor bastard sliced right past his distal, proximal, and metatarsals, and then past the medial cuneiforms to the navicular bone. Lots of panic and pain and blood, but we got the guys bandaged and stabilized and to the hospital.

Dave came in just before quitting time to get his hand freshly bandaged.

We'd worked together all the way to the lake and we'd blasted rock together for years. He was a driller. I considered him my best friend. And yet, we were different in many ways. In spite of his two years of art school before dropping out to make good money in construction, Dave wasn't in any sense a romantic. He didn't even remember women's names, just the clothing or hair color that made them distinct in his blurred bar scene memories of one-night stands. He'd say, "The chick with the white cutoffs," or "The one with the skin-tight tank top," or "The hottie with purple hair at Rockers last night," really basic hormonal stuff. In spite of his intelligence, Dave seemed to have zero interest in really connecting with any woman as a person. And based on his accounts of the women he had banged, none of them showed any desire for a real connection with any man. Male or female it was just booze it up, get laid, and move on.

We were different. I remember once when we'd had a few beers after work in camp, in fact it was the day I shot that grizzly in self-defense, I probed our friendship by confiding in him and sharing my memories of kissing Sally, of her mystical fresh mouth, and how the memory of her mouth was vividly evoked with every load of dynamite we detonated while building the road to Vermilion Lake. Dave gave me a long serious look when I'd finished my self-revelation, and then burst out laughing, absolutely sure that I was trying to tell him some kind of idiotic joke. I grinned and swigged back on my beer and permanently left it at that.

Dave's hand was slightly swollen and it needed a thorough cleaning with Bactine, but he didn't need a tetanus shot, and I wrapped him up with fresh bandages. Once I was done, he asked me if I wanted to hit the new bar in town, apparently there was "a lot of hot tail up there" according to rumor, and as always I said, "I'll pass man. I'm in training." I was a regular in the company fitness center. That excuse always worked.

After shaving and showering and throwing on fresh jeans and a white T-shirt, I left my trailer around 8:30 p.m. and headed towards the lake trail. The setting sun was a soft fiery red and the sky was streaked with purple gashes. The surface of the lake was perfect, pinkish-silver calm glass, and as I walked down to the edge of the lake I thought of Johnny's comment about "our bench." With the street lights sparkling uphill to my right, and the smooth lake surface on my left, and the brushed concrete trail under me, I felt like I was approaching an intersection point in the setting Johnny had created for Vermilion Lake. It took about ten minutes to see the bench in the distance and a person sitting there.

As I got closer, I saw Johnny, but she looked different. She had come to the bench straight from a late meeting with Will New, and she was dressed in a formal dark-blue business suit with jacket and knee-length skirt. She was wearing a stark-white buttoned blouse and her bare legs were slipped into black high heels. Her red hair was up in an extremely formal looking bun without a strand free. I'd not seen her with glasses the night before and she looked very scholarly. She stood up as I approached, and said, "Hi Tom," and gave me a gentle hug. As I held her for a second against my chest I could feel her soft breasts through the layers of her suit, and the scent of her hair was beautiful, and then she stepped back and said, "Please sit down. We've got a lot to discuss."

The whole scene felt very different from the previous night. And from this meeting onwards I wouldn't quite know what to make of Johnny. She was about to become a character composed of incongruous pieces, sometimes strong, sometimes fragile—almost patient-like. It was as if she had fallen apart and some force was in the process of reassembling her as a beautiful mess.

"Tom, last night I was shocked by my reaction to you. I felt a lot of feelings that I didn't expect," she said.

"Me too," I said with a smile, but she responded with a serious face, "Please let me finish, Tom." And so I shut up.

"You might think I'm a freak, but I need to tell you right now that I am a virgin and I believe in until death do us part marriage. I know that makes me look crazy, but it's true. If we end up getting married, it will be in the Catholic Church and our kids will be raised Catholic. That's not negotiable."

Stunned, I tried to open my mouth, but she carefully put her right index finger on my lips and said, "Just listen, please," and so I shut up again.

"I'm okay with being a freak, Tom. I'm a highly educated idealistic medieval freak and I might die alone old and gray in my bed, but that is who I am. And yes, I obviously sublimate my desires into my work, I know I do, and that's okay too because that is who I am."

I tried to respond again, but there was that pretty index finger with the light blue nail polish and minute star decorations against my lips again, and this time she kept it there as she continued. And it felt good with her keeping it there.

"If and only if we get married will we have sex, Tom. Let that be clear right now. You're a healthy handsome man and it's only fair to make that clear to you before we go any further."

It was incredibly sexy to have her say this to me while holding her finger on my lips. It seemed surreal, like something you'd hear in a movie, not real life. And there was no smiling or confused signals here. Johnny meant business, and she was laying down reality for me. She was authoritative and bold, but also extremely cute and outrageous.

"Also," she said, and then removed her finger from my lips and sat back into the bench in an erect posture, "We need to see our situation objectively and be rational about our future, whether we end up as man and wife, just friends, or dissolve forever out of each other's lives. And so our top priority must be clarifying your relationship with my sister. And until that is done, there can be no us. And so, no more hugs, no more dreamy talks, no more touching of any kind, and especially we must be vigilant about kissing: we must not kiss."

I smiled widely, but she immediately shut me down and said in all seriousness, "I'm serious, Tom. Last night I kept looking at your handsome face, your eyes, the shape of your mouth, the rugged bone structure of your jaw, and then your mouth again, and even as I tried to sleep, I kept thinking about your lips. I'm afraid that if I give in and kiss you an explosion of feelings will overwhelm me and I'll become selfish. That wouldn't be fair to my sister. Do you understand?"

That was my cue to talk and I said, "I think you're right. I need to see Sally as soon as possible."

And with that said, Johnny finally smiled and started to relax, and then said with a sigh, "What a day. I've been so stressed about how you'd react."

Then she removed her glasses and slipped them into her suit's breast pocket, loosened her top blouse buttons so she could breathe freely, and removed the jeweled pins holding up her bright red hair and let it fall and shook it out and stroked it into place over her breasts and fluffed it over her back. With a huge relaxed smile she reminded me, "Remember now, Tom, we're revving our engines with the brakes on. Only God knows if the NHRA Christmas Tree will work and the green light will flash on."

"You realize how good you look, eh?" I said. And she responded with a smile, "You realize how good you look, eh?"

"Don't worry, Tom, God will give us the strength to overcome millions of years of hormonal evolution," she said with an unconsciously formal tone.

I wasn't sure about God, but I replied, "So we're harnessed in funny cars at the starting line, the crowd is tense, our engines are roaring, and we're watching the Christmas Tree waiting for the green light so we can floor it and haul back on our LENCO C S1 transmissions and blast down the track chasing Vic Potens' 369 mph record time for the quarter mile?"

"You've done your research," she said with a smile. I smiled back.

"So where is your sister? I'll call her."

"I wish it was that easy. I'm worried, because Sally left to visit convents and sister houses in Quebec three months ago—Dad's influence on us girls was strong. He had almost become a Benedictine monk before he met Mom, and he always respected that lifestyle. Interspersed with his Motown hits he'd play Gregorian chant records from Fontgombault. As kids we absorbed that stuff—and although Sally isn't planning on becoming a nun or anything, she wants to experiment with their lifestyle, just enjoy being medieval inside for a while. She said she'd be spending a few days at different convent guest houses, but she hasn't stayed in touch like she promised."

"Not even a text message?" I asked.

"No. Part of her medieval thing is disdain towards technology, no cell phone, no Facebook, no Twitter, no Instagram. She's become a sort of monastic hipster / Luddite hybrid, but she said she would call every two weeks using a landline phone. She hasn't done that."

It was now around 9:30 p.m. and the sky in front of us glowed a fluorescent pink along the sharp mountains surrounding the lake. Above us the sky was darkening and thousands of stars were emerging. The air was still and cool; an occasional walker passed by us, and a few cars hummed above us up on the main drag. The car show crowd was gone and the street was empty.

"Have you called the police," I asked.

"After four weeks, yes. I didn't call earlier because I didn't want to panic in case she was spending solitary time in a hermitage or something. The police haven't found her, Tom, and I really need you to help me hunt her down, for her safety's sake, but also for us too. Okay?"

"Absolutely. How do we begin?"

"We need to find the websites for all of the contemplative orders in Quebec, not the active orders. She was only interested in the contemplatives. Then we'll each take half of the list and start contacting them."

Johnny explained that contemplative sisters devoted all of their time to prayer, and were not active in hospital ministries or education. We agreed that she'd get the list finished by morning; then we'd each take half and see if we could come up with anything on Sally's whereabouts. There couldn't be many contemplatives left, Johnny said, so it shouldn't take us long to contact them. We could probably get it done by tomorrow after work and meet again at the bench at nine, if not earlier.

"I'll walk you to your motel," I said, now that our plan was in place.

It was getting darker and cool and Johnny buttoned her blouse closed to the neck and started to put her hair up in a bun, but this time it was a messy bun with red wisps escaping over her eyes and ears. She adjusted her skirt and stood up. We both were visibly awkward because we knew that within the next twenty-four hours our futures could be changed forever.

"Let's see where this takes us, Tom. I'll text you your list of contacts in the morning."

"Sounds good," I said, and raising my empty hand in the air as if holding a glass, I motioned that we toast, "To the mystery of destiny."

She touched her invisible glass to mine and said, "To the mystery of providence," and smiled.

I walked her up to Gold Motel and left her without a hug, only a warm glance. I watched her move through the yellow neon glow into her motel room. I heard her door click secure, saw the ember light come on, and walked alone through the streets back to my trailer and what would be a night of dreams.

CHAPTER FOUR:

I took a shower and crashed. I was thinking of Johnny's wisps of hair, then the morning list and how I'd word my inquiries, then how many there would be, then Johnny's green eyes with her glasses on, then how long it would take to hear back, and fragments of what ifs and what ifs like silent waves pulsating towards me until I sank into a deep sleep.

A miniscule candle seemed to burn in a distant calm darkness, then another closer by, then hundreds surrounding a large bright white bed. A white lit room. Then an overwhelming warm softness and my eyes closed and slowly reopened. Sally was under me in aching, naked anticipation. Together unclothed on that bright sheet we slowly kissed and barely touched along each other's ribs and thighs and arms, all the while kissing slowly and delicately and wetly, both of us aching with anticipation of consummation. Sally's bright blue eyes were looking into mine, and her glossy black hair spread like soft lace over the pillow under her beautiful head and her smile of absolute trust. The flames around us were purifying and lifting our pleasure towards some mystery; our arousal was synchronized and rising in intensity. And then an abrupt darkness, a sudden huff that blackened the candles and left the room smelling of smoldering wicks, then a warm dissolving and I was alone on my back in absolute night, in pure darkness staring at the flat-black ceiling.

Then I was getting out of the Shelby to open the door for Johnny and working my way through the crowd pressing around the car to the door and then pulling on the door handle but it was locked and I looked in and the Shelby was empty and the crowd pushed me along like driftwood during spring thaw on a northern steelhead river, and then the Shelby dissolved into a tangle of neon veins and colors and then darkness, and I was alone on the bed in silence, and then above me a soft glow of pink light and then slowly and gently, out of the thin black air Johnny appeared floating in a gravity pulling against me, firmly against the ceiling, she was clothed in an ethereal pale-green diaphanous garment wafting in the still indoor air, then motionless she was slowly lowered as if with wires to within inches of my naked body, her cool fresh breath gentle on my face, not strands but cascades of her red hair silky in my face and over my shoulders and chest, she was smiling and looking at me with her pure green eyes, and then I saw that not wires, but thickly feathered large golden wings extending from her shoulders in gentle motion were holding her in midair.

And I thought to myself, What the hell?

And then she hovered a bit higher and her breasts were succulent in the gravity under her sheer gauze. I lay there absorbing her until I moved my tongue and tasted Sally's delicious mouth from the previous dream.

Then I saw a big buck mounting a doe during the rut and I woke up.

I decided I would keep this dream to myself. Dave would think I was an idiot. I lay there until the alarm went off at 6:00 a.m. and then got up and showered off the sweat. Like the day before, my phone was vibrating on the windowsill. The hot morning sun was pushing through slivers of space in the curtains and I grabbed my phone and read the text: "Tom, here's your share of the list. God be with you." And Johnny had three links below, under which she wrote, "See you around nine at the bench." "The bench," I said aloud to myself, and wrote back, "Absolutely."

That day my first-aid station was quiet in the morning and I had time to open the links Johnny had sent me. Lots of religious pictures and phrases that seemed strange to me to be sure, but each site was clearly laid out in distinct sections. And each site had a RETREAT INFORMATION button for potential visitors to click on. I tried these buttons, but I was overwhelmed with strange details about vigils and feasts and processions and fasts, so I just went to the CONTACT buttons and decided to phone long distance and get it done.

First, I called Sister Bernadette at The Convent of Our Lady of Perpetual Help in Aspireh, Quebec. After being transferred through two aging female voices, I finally heard a younger bubbly voice say, "This is Sister Bernadette, God bless you. How can I help you?"

I answered, "Sister, this is Thomas Tems calling from Vermilion Lake Village in B.C. Could you please tell me if a Sally Nostal is visiting your convent right now, or perhaps was there recently? Her sister and I are trying to contact her."

She asked if she could put me on hold while she checked the guest registry, and I said, "Of course, thank you."

Pre-recorded angelic-sounding nuns sang Gregorian chant for a few minutes and then Sister Bernadette came back on the line and said, "No one by that name is here now, and our residence sister, Sister Mariana, says she's never heard of her. She's not contacted us. I'm so sorry."

"Thank you for trying, Sister."

"God bless your search, Thomas. I trust she is safely in God's hands somewhere. I'll ask Our Lady to help you."

I said, "Thank you. Goodbye, Sister," not knowing what "Our Lady" helping might really mean. I didn't grow up in this terrain as the Nostal sisters had, and certainly my secular college years didn't map it for me.

The second call was to Sister Carmella at The Hermitage of St. John of the Cross in Labellecruz. A very old female voice slowly answered, "Sister Carmella." And then a silence.

I responded, "Sister Carmella," and speaking slowly and clearly in case her hearing was impaired, I said, "This is Thomas Tems calling from B.C."

She quickly cut me off, "I'm sorry but you must have the wrong number. We are nuns here at a hermitage. There are no men here. God bless you," and she began to hang up.

"Wait please, Sister," I said, and explained the purpose of my call.

Sister Carmella listened carefully to my explanation and then put me on hold as she went to inquire of the sisters about Sally. This time there was only silence, punctuated with the occasional taps of footsteps passing the phone, for at least ten minutes before Sister Carmella picked up again.

She said, "Thomas," and then waited to see if I was still there on the line, and I answered, "Yes, Sister." Then she began, "Sister Angelica tells me that Sally did contact us about four months ago. She requested a cabin in our forest for one week. Like all of us she was planning to devote herself to solitary prayer for six days and then join the community for Mass on Sunday. Apparently, Sister Angelica has corresponded with her frequently and she was excited to visit us. But she never arrived."

"Never arrived. Do you know why, Sister?"

"No. Sister Angelica said she tried to contact her but she received no responses."

"No responses at all?"

"None, Thomas. But I am confident that she is in God's hands. I will pray for her, and I'll also ask our patron to intercede for her, perhaps she is in the dark night of the senses."

I said, "Thank you," and hung up, oblivious to her dark night of the senses comment, but glad to have had at least a spark of luck with Sally's name. She was somewhere. Somewhere silent, I suspected.

My last contact was Sister Augustina at The Convent of Saint Monica. Just as I was about to call her, Mike Davis, one of the young framing carpenters working in the East Edge section of the project, burst in shirtless, cursing with his bloody hand wrapped in his white T-shirt.

"Fucking idiot! Son of a bitch!" he moaned as he pumped his wounded hand in the air.

I calmed him down and washed up the wound with Bactine. As he settled, Mike said he'd let his mind wander while he was hammering 4 inch spiral nails into 2 x 4 s. He took his mind off a nail and drove it through both his left middle and ring fingers, scraping the 3rd and 4th proximal flanges and nailing his hand to the wall he was erecting.

"Son of a fucking bitch," he sighed, and shook his darkly tanned head in disgust at himself.

"Lucky the nail was bright and not galvanized," I said.

Now that I'd rinsed off the blood and sawdust with antiseptic, I could assess how badly both fingers were ripped up by the spike. No flesh had been torn free nor blood vessels severed, and I decided that with good dressings he'd heal up without an emergency visit. He said he was thinking about a young woman he'd met at The Lightning Lounge the previous night. He couldn't remember her name, just her face and her pink tank top and that she was drinking Singapore Slings. As I positioned the aluminum-foam finger splints and applied the sterile pads and started wrapping the sterile gauze he smiled at me and said, quoting the Dierks Bentley country lyric, "I know what I was feelin', but what was I thinkin'?"

"Sounds like true love," I said smiling back.

And he replied, "That little pink tank top was true love, all right!"

When I finished bandaging Mike's hand, he got up and walked out of my first-aid station with a kind of 'I can handle anything' swagger that starkly contrasted with his panicky entrance.

I was about to call Sister Augustina when my cell vibrated and I saw a text from Johnny. She had contacted the convents on her list and none of them had heard of Sally. She had drawn a blank. She asked if I'd had any success: "Have any of the sisters heard from her?" I decided to call Sister before answering Johnny's message.

A young happy voice said, "The Convent of Saint Monica, Sister Augustina speaking."

I introduced myself and explained my purpose as I had before, and when she put me on hold the angelic voices of men and women singing Gregorian chant in harmony clicked on. I didn't know that this was even allowed. There was a kind of masculine beauty woven with a kind of feminine beauty. It was like particle physics or something. I don't know. I listened for probably fifteen minutes before the phone went dead and a dial tone kicked in.

"What the hell?" I said aloud and called the number again.

I let it ring about twenty times, then hung up again, redialled and tried again letting it ring for a long time, and then the same again, but no one answered. I grabbed a coffee and called again. This time Sister Augustina picked up the phone. She recognized my voice and apologized for losing our connection. She said her retreat records showed that Sally had contacted them about four months ago and she was scheduled to stay for three days, but after that first contact, she never followed up. She seemed to have changed her mind, Sister speculated.

I thanked her, and she said, "God bless you, Thomas. The Saints will help you find her," and hung up.

I texted Johnny: "Two places have heard from her, but not seen her. I'll explain in detail at the bench."

"At six, not nine, if possible," Johnny texted back, and I responded, "Sounds good," understanding her urgency.

After lunch, two more injuries came in, one a scraped ear, the other a finger injury. A guy had zapped a screw into his left index finger with an air drill, said it happened in a split second, and when he saw the head of the screw flush with his finger tip—the zap had spiraled the full length of the screw along the distal and middle phalanges of his index finger—he stared at what he'd done in disbelief, but then had the sense to put the drill in reverse and zap the damn thing out as fast as it went in. "Then the blood started to piss out," he said. And that was good because it cleaned the wound. Neither of the two guys blamed thinking about women as the cause of his injury, and I basically cleaned them both up with Bactine, bandaged them and got them on their way. Around 3:00 p.m. I heard a helicopter pass overhead towards the East Edge development of the lake. I didn't think much of it until around 4:00 p.m. when Dave came in for a fresh bandage.

As I was cleaning up his hand with Bactine, he said, "Do you remember Roy Backer?"

"The surveyor from our road crew? Sure."

"Last week, Roy told me at The Lightning that behind the properties they're framing on the East Edge they've had boulders come down right into the work areas. 'Some big bastards,' he said. He told his foreman, but the foreman said there might be a few loose rocks, but not to worry, 'The slopes are safe.'"

"Safe all right. A chopper just flew Roy out of there to Prince George emergency! Did you hear it go over?"

"That was for Roy?"

"Yeah. He was framing a door on the main floor and out of nowhere a huge rock hit him in the head. He might die. It was bad."

"Son of a bitch. I hope the doctors can help him."

"Yeah."

There was a silence. Then as I started to wrap fresh gauze over Dave's sterile pad he said, "Roy's accident reminds me of that young woman who got hurt in the blast. Remember, just as we were finishing the road in here?"

"What young woman?"

"You know, the one who got hurt just as we were finishing the road in here."

"Hurt? You told me that she was killed, Dave. You said she was 'unrecognizable ... gone.' Those were your words."

"That was the story I got, but later Mike said he talked to some nurses at Prince George emergency and they said they saw her come in, crushed to hell for sure, no memory, a bunch of shit wrong, but for sure not dead."

"The young woman in the metallic-green Bronco? Are you sure, Dave? I mean really sure?"

"Yeah, I'm sure. Mike and I partied with those nurses. I can't remember my nurse's name, she was the one with the unbelievable face, but we partied at The Lightning Lounge just after the accident and she wouldn't shut up about her. Said she wished she had her blue eyes and teeth."

"Blue eyes and teeth? Sensitive nurse," I said. "Do you know if she's still at Prince George Hospital?"

"The nurse?"

"No, the young woman who didn't die!"

"Yeah, she is. Don't laugh, but I've been visiting her. I figured if that nurse with the unbelievable face was jealous, she must be welding torch hot and I should drop by to visit."

"You've been hitting on a patient in emergency? That's incredible, Dave. I've got to rethink our friendship, man. That's brutal."

"It was the nurse's idea, not mine. I figured if I went I might score again with that nurse, you know."

"But that nurse is history now, so why have you kept going to visit?"

"She *is* red hot, and her wounds are healing fast, and she's different. The doctors say her memory is gone. It was blasted blank when our rocks hit her, but now her mind is clearing and she seems to really care about me, Tom."

"Dave Casanova, the one-night stand man, the king of no names, the king of hit and run, are you kidding me? Since when do you care if a woman cares?"

"Remember when you shot that grizzly, the day you told me that idiotic joke about the fantasy woman's lips?"

"Yeah, but for the record it was her entire mouth, not just her lips."

"Well, I guess I'm becoming an idiot. I know this sounds stupid, but we kissed for the first time during my last visit, and I swear the wall nearly blew out of the hospital wing!"

"What the hell?"

"Seriously. I don't know if it was her gum or what, but her mouth was like an explosion. As our wet lips met and I tasted her tongue, the rush reminded me of the dynamite we detonated as we drilled and blew our way into this valley."

"You're nuts, man."

"I can't remember how many women I've kissed, Tom, but this is different. I'm addicted to her. I have no choice but to keep going back for more. Sally is special."

"Sally?"

"Yeah, she doesn't remember, but the nurses say that's the name on her ID."

"I've got to make a call, Dave."

I finished taping up his bandage and rushed him out of my station. I phoned Johnny and said, "I think I've got some real news. Can we meet right now? I can get George to fill in for my last hour here." She said she could get away in ten minutes when the meeting ended and she'd be right down to our bench.

CHAPTER FIVE:

Above our bench the sky was an empty pure blue, and there was no wind at all. Vermilion Lake was a placid silvery-blue sheet. I sat there in my work clothes, a few sprinkles of blood on my shirt pocket and right pant leg. Behind me and back up the hill on the lake-edge main drag, the car show was in its third day and the murmur of the visitors and faint clunking sounds of doors and hoods opening were background soundtrack. My mind was racing. If Dave's Sally is our Sally, what then? If her memory will return in time, what then? If the sister and lover are gone forever, what then?

There was no track. Time seemed to be frozen for the mint condition hot rods up behind me in the show—old cars preserved like new, better even than new, polished with diaper flannel like high-end ultra-accurate Sako sniper rifles, delicately loved and treasured; every detail of every car clean, dry, perfectly painted, every part authentic, original, perfectly restored, or custom blown out for strength and power, and the quality mufflers purring and holding down the rage of the muscular V-8s, the stereos and furry rugs and pink dice dangling. And Sally long ago in that Vancouver alley in the Shelby, and Johnny yesterday in that Shelby up on the hill, and all of the guys and girls and memories in cars since the motors started in the early factories; and I closed my eyes and rested them and saw the two Nostal sisters in the two Shelbys parked side by side at the Dairy Queen and the two Toms, one younger and one older, looking across at each other smiling and giving the thumbs up, meaning hot ride dude and hot chick and life doesn't get any better and better click the shutter on this picture because you'll need it when the pain and chaos break in, or the good memories kick in, or the best keeps being the best and you drag race through life without a scratch, or whatever, or concussions bang out of nowhere and you're thrown from the car, or roll cages and flames, or married with daughters and Motown and Chant and full-sleeve tattoos.

I heard light clicking steps and opened my eyes and came back to Johnny sitting down next to me on the bench. The sky was slowly becoming slightly pinkish and Johnny looked formal and intelligent in burnt orange with white and an emerald pendant and serious green eyes and love. She held out her right hand to me and held mine and said, "Tell me what you've discovered, Tom."

"When Dave came in for a fresh bandage today, he told me a story that seems incredible, but it makes sense. Don't panic, but I'm pretty sure she's nearby in Prince George Hospital's extended care unit."

"Hospital! Not at a convent? What do you mean? Are you sure?"

"No, I definitely am not sure, but Dave's story sounds like it might be her. His description of her and the timing seem to fit Sally's disappearance."

"What do you mean?"

I waited to answer as two joggers ran past our bench.

"A young woman was injured—I thought killed—as we were finishing up the blasting to get in here to the lake. It happened at the time you said Sally left. Two of the Sisters I contacted said they heard from Sally back then, but she never showed."

I paused as a lone jogger passed by; then we were alone.

"All I can guess is that maybe she tried to find me before going back east, but then had the accident. I don't know, but we've got to check this out. Dave claims she is healing quickly but has no memory and that she is his girlfriend now!"

"My sister is your friend Dave's girlfriend? He's a chaste Catholic I hope?"

Obviously I knew what the word chaste meant, but I'd never heard it actually used in a conversation before.

"Not quite. But he claims he's transforming, going through some kind of metamorphosis. That's why we've got to get to Prince George to meet her. There is something very different about this young woman, whoever she is."

"And if it is Sally?"

"Then it is Sally, and we'll watch the lights move on the NHRA Christmas Tree," I said and smiled.

"How far is it?"

"It's about a two hour drive. Can you get tomorrow off? Or maybe stay for a fifth day?"

"Will New and I wrapped up our discussions today. I'm free to leave in the morning, early."

"I'll get George to fill in for me tomorrow and we can leave at 7:00 a.m. Okay? I can borrow a company pickup for the day."

"That will be good," Johnny replied, and then sighed a nervous breath. "If it is her, I hope she is all right."

"For sure. It's been interesting meeting you, Ms. Nostal."

"And you too, Mr. Tems."

I grinned and said, "Does what we're going through make any sense to you? I mean in light of your architectural theory for this lake."

"I don't know, Tom. I never really imagined my concept as literally being true. It was more of a romantic hope. I know this might sound archaic, but I really thought of it as a deeply intellectual kind of medieval feminine hope. Like I said, I'm not afraid of the freak label. I'll never forget a professor's comment on one of my university essays—an essay in a Chaucer course. He wrote, 'You have a remarkable grasp of the medieval worldview.' What a wonderful comment. I was describing my current worldview in the essay. It was refreshing to know I got it right."

Johnny thrust up her arms and gestured like a referee signaling a touchdown, and laughed.

She then added, "When I first saw the aerial photos of the lake and saw it was heart shaped, I was struck. And when I saw the glaciers fusing into Windhover Creek in the north and entering the lake and then exiting through the southern end of the lake, I imagined the icy current of melted snow forming a diagonal arrow through the lake and visualized a tree with the initials of lovers in the center. It was like an illuminated manuscript in my mind. I thought of this place," and she motioned to the view before us as the sky was fully a warm pink now, "as the romantic equivalent of the Bermuda Triangle. A place where beautiful storms and accidents could occur, storms of love, not sorrow, Tom. But maybe the two breathe together. I don't know."

Worrying about Sally was weighing heavily upon Johnny, so to lighten up I asked, "How does your storm theory mesh with the accuracy of Cupid's arrow? Surely, he's not just blasting projectiles in all directions."

"The accuracy of love?"

"Yeah. Accuracy. Wouldn't true lovers have to be in the exact place at the exact time, in the crosshairs of destiny to put it in modern terms?"

"Crosshairs?"

"Do you know what I'd add to your design for this place?" I said.

"What?"

"This is going to sound ridiculous and like a total guy thing, but hear me out. At the north end, facing towards the mountains and away from all of the developed residential lots, I'd install three 1000 yard target shooting ranges."

"Target shooting ranges! Really romantic. Why?"

"First, because the Swiss are obsessed with target shooting. Your company would love it. Second, it would be a huge draw for European investors who love shooting but currently find themselves in a shrinking setting where ranges are being forced to close because of noise complaints. And third and most important, the gun Zen of breathing, the delicate caress of the trigger, the precision and concentration of developing the perfect load culminating in an accurate explosion. Those ranges would offer romantic men the perfect combination of optimum internal ballistics, optimum external ballistics, and optimum terminal ballistics!"

"Optimum terminal ballistics! What are you talking about, Tom?"

"Accurate kisses that go BANG is what I'm talking about!"

"You're crazy, Tom. But sweet. I'll give it some serious thought and mention it to Will and see if he laughs or thinks I'm serious. Who knows, maybe he'll think you're right?"

A thin veil of black was slowly lowering over the pink sky and the lake was becoming a calm gunmetal color. Johnny's upper lip, the slightly turned up defiant upper edge of it, which seemed to be saying, "This lip doesn't get kissed yet," looked unbelievably, and I mean unbelievably, pretty. We individually walked up the cement path and headed back to her motel. We didn't hug; we just smiled and wished each other a good rest and agreed that tomorrow couldn't come too soon.

CHAPTER SIX:

That night I was blown away by a weird dream. The woman in it could have been either Sally or Johnny. I couldn't tell because the woman's face was a featureless glow. We were driving at night and our headlights lit a narrow forest-walled gravel road as it turned and pot-holed and opened into a campsite area. And there was a vast trough-like valley of thick stump bases glowing in the dim night light. It was Ross Lake reservoir in Skagit Valley Provincial Park, which in July is low on the Canadian side. In the headlights, we set up our house tent and slid into a warm darkness.

At dawn we saw "the pond," a seemingly endless field of massive stumps cut low, an entire valley clear-cut and sucked dry of life. Not one twig of green or bird nesting. Billions of weathered stump-rings facing the blue sky. The breathing and growth and stillness, the homes and paths of animals—excited squirrels radiant in their earth colors, aroused thick grizzlies, blood-red-headed wood peckers whacking bark, all objectively recorded, each life finished and unique and annihilated. In the extreme distance, the water was flat with glare and the pond swelled towards our shore, the countless stumps breaking the surface—rising towards us by degrees in perspective until at our shoreline they were fully routed and exposed.

Her face was an oblivious white glow. With the camp stove smells of delicious butter-fried eggs and fragrant bacon fading into the forest, and our tent zipped shut, and our car locked, holding hands we descended to explore the shore, climbing over cement-colored dead wood. The edge of the pond was cold as we inserted our warm feet. With the sun almost above us now in the empty sky, we searched for absolute privacy. I had our white flannel blanket over my left shoulder, careful not to let it get wet as it hung down. The hot sun glared and bent and sparked off the water; our feet glistened with clear beads melting off. In my head I heard our car radio blasting, "I can't get enough of your love. I can't get enough of your love." BAAAMMM BAAAMMM BAAAMMM BOP BOP!

Then we found our bed of clean sand. A half circle of massive worn stumps bordered by water, the sand billions of worn specks of stones pulverized by time and left by the ice age millennia ago. She stood there against the base of a once huge shaft. I gazed down her slightly open white blouse and saw the cool shadows cast by her breasts. Our white blanket floated onto the sand between the trees whose seeds had germinated deep in the moist earth beneath our feet hundreds of years before we were conceived. Then she laid her body down and motioned me to join her. Then a cool breeze swirled softly. She wanted us to explode this beach off of the map, no, explode it off of the galaxy. She could hear me singing the blues classic "King Bee." Then she saw me pull back from the microphone and play a palmated blues progression while the solo wounded us all.

And then ... in the silent sun, in the silent cool breeze, with the lake submitting silently to the harsh stump terrain's thousands of years of fertility truncated by an abruptly halted colossal hydro project bizarrely deemed a pond—it was our time. And then we made love and made love until ... FLASH ... our feet were pulled through the sand and down into the moist earth and BOOOOOMM honey blasted like missiles out of the silos of the stumps and thousands of severed trunks rocketed into the sky and the earth burst with rushing colors and billions of plants and creatures exploded into the sky and floated there high above us—hovering—the grizzlies, especially amongst the creatures, looking down stunned and absolutely shocked to be alive—as below we lay naked, satisfied in each other's arms, glowing, exhausted, married.

And then I woke up soaked in sweat. And then I showered.

At 7:00 a.m. sharp, I pulled the company truck into the visitor parking of Johnny's motel. She waved from her window and rushed out. She was wearing a white hoodie, white tank top, white jeans, and white sandals. Her hair was loose and down, but she had a thin crown-like medieval-looking braid which wound around her head to the back and allowed her forehead to be clear. She carried by its strap a pink backpack and hopped into the truck and looked at me and smiled and took a deep breath and said, "Let's go meet her."

It was a strange drive because I had been so busy with work that I had never driven the road out of Vermilion Lake Village. What took us so long to blast through, only took 45 minutes at 70 mph to drive over. Lots of thoughts. The healed edges of the road were thick with thrown boulders and scattered Ponderosa pines until we descended and the road was then lined with succulent cacti and low-growing desert plants.

After a few minutes, Johnny said, "It must have been a lot of work to build this road, Tom."

And I replied, "Yeah. It took a lot of dynamite."

When we reached the Highway #3 junction, we took the northern branch and were on our way to the hospital.

The silence was awkward, and I said to Johnny, "Please forgive me for not talking, I've just got a lot on my mind."

"Me too," she said, and we agreed to listen to music while we drove.

Johnny pulled a stack of CDs out of her backpack and smiled, "Classic Motown, Tom. What do you say we kick it off with The Temptations' 'My Girl'"?

"Go for it," I responded and adjusted the treble and bass, and then we heard, "I've got sunshine on a cloudy day," and Johnny and I were feeling good as we drove on. Just before 9:00 a.m., we saw the blue capital **H** hospital sign on the outskirts of Prince George, and by 9:15 a.m. the hospital was in sight in the distance.

CHAPTER SEVEN:

I shut off the music and looked across at Johnny and said, "There it is," and she responded, "Yeah," and was visibly pensive. For some reason, I flashed back to my college years and thought of Jonathan as he approached Dracula's castle perched on that horrific precipice, ancient and solitary with its interminable labyrinth of hallways of locked doors and the winding darkness Jonathan nervously carved through with his flickering candles, and all of the ancient scars and secrets somehow imprisoned forever there in those walls. We stopped at the first of three lights before the large hospital entrance sign. It was visible ahead, above us, as the hill ascended.

A heavily tattooed young man walked past us as we waited for the light to change. He was like me, about five foot ten, but with a clean-shaved head, single earring, slit shades, Foo Manchu, black singlet, and massive arms tattooed to his wrists—he was a mobile mural in tight black jeans with a silver wallet chain dangling and pointed black cowboy boots. He glanced at us for a second with metallic blue eyes as he walked confidently in the crosswalk carrying his baby daughter against his heart in a sling—her pink bonnet, like a blossom in the morning sun, scorching a path for them both. Johnny glanced at me and smiled softly. The light changed, and as I pressed down on the gas I flashed back to my college years again and thought of Kafka's character K showing up at the castle entrance only to be turned away and back into a local hotel to begin an endless cycle of bureaucratic tangles culminating in a truncation of the narrative with K carrying a box of papers in a meaningless hallway. A land surveyor paralyzed indoors.

Then Johnny brought me back with a pop by saying, "Tom, have you ever read St. Theresa of Avilla's *The Interior Castle*?

"Castle?" I said surprised. "No, what made you think of that now?"

"It just hit me that if Sally is here in the hospital, and if it's true that she has irretrievable memory loss, then she might be moving inwards to the deepest room at the core of the castle of her soul."

"Sounds medieval. Is that good?" I asked.

"For St. Theresa it is for sure, because that most secret and protected inner room is where the light of God's presence dwells. If you can work your way through the halls to that door and open it, you will find peace," she said and smiled hopefully.

"There's the turnoff at the next light, Tom."

I steered the truck left and drove down a bit and into the hospital parking lot. The hospital signs were clear and we headed to the south end of the lot, closest to the extended care entrance sign, and parked. I backed the truck into a space at the furthest edge because I can't stand backing out of parking lots. I'm not confident about judging distances in a pickup with an 8 foot box, and I always prefer to drive straight out so I can see where I'm going. I explained this to Johnny, and she gave me a quizzical look.

On the trip up, we'd agreed that we'd first go to the nursing station and explain who we were and our speculation that one of their patients might be Johnny's sister. Once that was done we'd ask about her memory and physical condition, and then ask them to let us check from a distance to confirm her identity, and then if it was Sally, we'd ask them to please give us a bit of time to think and gather ourselves before actually visiting her.

The extended care entrance was a modern, high-vaulted ceiling with a cedar log design framework holding huge panes of clear glass open to the sky above us. It was beautiful and so well-lit that it seemed almost sterile. The receptionist was about twenty steps inside the external sliding glass doors. We approached the desk and introduced ourselves to the receptionist who immediately directed us to the nursing window another fifteen paces along the bright hall. There, a nurse in her mid-thirties, with kind brown eyes and glossy black hair up in a blue cap like doctors wear during surgery, greeted us with, "Good morning, can I help you." Her name tag read *Anastasia*, and her face radiated a compassionate intelligence infused with years of witnessing suffering. I sensed she loved life. We told her our story, and Johnny explained that her sister's name was Sally. That perked Ana's attention and she immediately pulled a file from the shelf behind and to her right.

She flipped it open and studied and shuffled some papers and said, "This young woman survived a very traumatic accident about four months ago. A large statue packed tightly into the rear seating area behind the driver's seat prevented her from being killed by the rocks which crushed her vehicle."

Johnny held my arm and said, "gracia plena."

The nurse looked puzzled at Johnny's spontaneous Latin, then continued, "There was also a fire at the scene. Fortunately, it never reached the patient, but it did destroy some of the vehicle's contents. The vehicle had no plates or registration papers, and the young woman's driver's license was melted except for a fragment of the corner where we could read the name Sally, but no more. We reported her to the RCMP as a missing person, and you are the first hope we've seen so far."

Johnny and I were hopeful, and Ana agreed to let us see her from a distance. She asked another nurse to take her place at the station while she showed us to the ward. The patient was in Room 49 and she recommended that we take seats in the common visiting room while she went in and encouraged Sally to take a slow walk down the hall with her as she explained some of the new medications her doctor was considering. We could hear their faint voices, and Johnny gripped my arm in seeming recognition, and then Ana and Sally gingerly emerged and turned down the disinfected hall and walked slowly towards us. We both recognized Sally instantly and Johnny took my hand in hers and whispered, "Pater noster, qui es in caelis," and said, "Tom, look at me, just talk to me quietly," and we both looked into each other's eyes as Sally and Ana did their brief lap, Ana seeing our confirmation and so shortening their lap and getting Sally back to her room gradually. And just above a whisper I said to Johnny, "It's going to be okay." "Yes," she sighed almost silently.

Ana soon came out of Room 49 and we approached her and then walked together down the granite-colored linoleum hall. She asked if we could "confirm," and we said, "Yes, we can confirm," to which she replied that she'd contact Dr. Joyce Willings, Sally's specialist, and see if we could talk to her immediately.

Ana buzzed her and we could, and she sent us straight up the elevator to Dr. Willings' office on the third floor. As we stood within the chrome-trimmed maroon inner walls of the elevator and felt the upward pull of the hidden cable above us, we looked across into each other's eyes.

Dr. Willings was intelligent and really lovely. She surprised me. Seeing her reminded me of when I was fourteen and I had to go for kidney x-rays. (It turned out they were fine.) I was lying on the cold stainless steel table with my bare back against the metal, and as a male nurse came in to prep me, I glanced over at the counter across from me and saw what looked like a syringe with a one pint barrel filled with milky white fluid and a needle around 3 inches long, and I said to him, "That's not for me is it?" To which he replied, "Yes, that's the dye we need to inject into you before the x-ray can be taken." Shit, I thought to myself, as I contemplated getting up and leaving. But then a beautiful, dark-haired Spanish doctor entered the room and asked me if I was ready, and I said, "Whenever you are, doctor." There was no way in hell that I was going to wimp out in front of a literally gorgeous woman. I'd die on that table first. I'll never forget how—as she was slowly pushing the plunger on the syringe and filling me with the fluid—she said with a gentle smile, "You might feel a little pressure, a little fullness as I inject the dye." Understatement of the century. It felt like the top of my head was going to blow off and my eyeballs burst as I gasped for breath and lied, "No problem, I'm fine."

Dr. Willings' dark auburn hair was pulled up into a formal bun, and she had warm brown eyes behind black thin-rimmed glasses. Her mouth was beautiful, and she was dressed in black slacks and a white blouse and a brilliant white doctor's coat. She welcomed us to sit down and with sincere joy said, "So our mystery patient has finally been found." She asked if we'd met her yet, and she was relieved when we said, "No, we've just seen her from a distance." She then explained Sally's condition, turned her large computer screen towards us, and showed us numerous color slides, brain scans, and charts, and explained that Sally's memory would never return, that was absolutely certain, but miraculously she had fully recovered from the concussion she had sustained and there was no reason she couldn't build a new and happy life from scratch. She also clarified, "You'll have to be very patient, because Sally will perceive you as complete strangers. You'll have to gain her confidence gradually by showing her evidence of who you are through videos and photographs from the past and legal documents like birth certificates and licenses."

Sitting there in her brightly lit office, open to the skyline through large ceiling to floor glazing edged with stainless steel, Johnny and I looked at each other and reached for each other's hands.

Also, she explained, "It will be up to you to create Sally's past, including whatever you feel will help her new life, and delete anything which will only confuse or depress her. It will be an ominous task," she explained, "but also an exciting construction project."

"Construction project," Johnny repeated aloud.

"Yes. Her past life is largely now in your hands. She will need a foundation to build her future on, and her past is your construction project."

Dr. Willings explained that although Sally would require weekly medical checkups and sessions with a psychologist in the future, she was fine for now and ready to go home as soon as that could be arranged.

"When would you like to meet her and begin?" she asked.

"Could Tom and I have a couple of hours to discuss things and then meet her today?"

"Certainly," she replied, "Why don't we meet her at 1:00 p.m. after lunch? I'll introduce you to her and stay with you until you want me to leave the room and give you some privacy. Then we can debrief back at my office and get your construction project underway."

"Wonderful," Johnny said, and we both stood up and headed for the elevator and down and out to the truck in the lot and to the nearest Subway the GPS led us to.

We were both hungry. I ordered a foot-long lightly toasted Italian bread meatball marinara sub with white cheese, avocado, lettuce, mayo, and lots of black olives, and a large chocolate milk to wash it down. When I was a kid, my mother voraciously wolfed down black olives. We'd buy them in bulk right out of the big oak brine barrels at Francesco's Italian Deli on Victoria Drive in Vancouver. I didn't like them as a boy, but as I matured I came to love them. Johnny ordered a six-inch tuna and lettuce with a large Coke. After eating, we both felt stronger.

"Top priority," I said to Johnny, "is that your sister's emotions for me and my emotions for her, never existed. If all of those years have been annihilated for good, then let it be. Do you agree?"

"Yes," Johnny said. "You can't recreate the past."

"She's your sister, Johnny. I won't interfere with your construction of her past, but practically speaking if I am to have never existed for her, then you'll have to be sure that any photograph, video, letter, diary entry, whatever, that includes me, must be destroyed."

"Destroyed? I understand your feelings Tom, but destroyed makes your relationship with Sally sound like it was a crime, and it was not a crime. It was beautiful."

"So what do you suggest?"

"How about something medieval?" she said and smiled as if a light had just switched on in her head.

"Meaning?"

"I suggest we physically remove all evidence of your relationship with Sally, and do so for her sake, and place it in a container. Have you read John Keats' long poem based on Boccaccio's story?"

"I have."

"Good, so nothing sad like a funeral urn or a pot of basil or anything. But instead, something like a small time capsule."

"And then? So she doesn't just find it and open it and have her life broken open?"

"Then perhaps bury it deep in a beautiful rose garden I could design and work into the landscaping plans for my lot at Vermilion."

"So a kind of mystical revision of that medieval story? No weeping. No broken hearts."

"Yeah. What do you think?"

"Hidden beauty. Deep under roses. I'll trust your judgement on that one. So that covers me, but where will she live?"

"My mom lives in South Bend, Indiana. She moved there to be close to us girls after Dad died and we were studying at Notre Dame. She could live with her in her apartment there. But to tell you the truth, Tom, I'd feel a lot better with her living with me at the lake, at least until she's strong and ready to move on. I could change my plans to include a special private suite for Sally where she could basically live in privacy. I could see her daily, but she'd have her own space, and I'm sure she'd love the lake."

"Sounds good for the future, but your place isn't even framed yet. Where will she live for the next few months? Not in my work trailer, that's for sure."

"Of course not, and living alone at Gold Motel while I'm back in New York would be useless too."

"And moving in with Dave wouldn't work."

"Moving in with Dave? No."

"Then where?"

"I think I need to take her back to my apartment in New York. There we can become sisters again, and with you out of the picture I'll be able to give her the past she needs to start fresh. Once my place is completed at the lake I'll move to Vermilion and work from home there with periodic flights to various project sites. Will New said my home could be completed within seven months. Once I move in, I can bury the capsule before the landscapers finish up."

"Are you sure it wouldn't be safer just to burn it all?"

"You don't burn the best in life, Tom."

"Okay, so your future plans are in place with me out of the picture. I guess here is where I mention that if in the future you ever have any interest in me as a man, I'll be at the lake bandaging builders for at least the next two years," I said and smiled at her clear thinking which no doubt was fueled by that tuna sub and big pop.

"Any interest?" she asked.

Then with her delicate hand she reached to my stubbly chin and drew my face close to hers, and placed her lips within a thousandth's of an inch from mine, and hovered there, a few miniscule particles of bread crumbs on her lips against mine, and then wispily licked my lower lip and then pressed her perfect wet mouth against mine and full on kissed me like she meant it and then pulled back and smiled widely and like Mount St. Helens the wall of the Subway blew out sideways, and I had my answer.

CHAPTER EIGHT:

We were back at Dr. Willings' office at 12:50 p.m., ready to meet Sally. She walked us down to Room 49, tapped on the door, and when Sally said, "Hello," the three of us entered. Sally was in bed watching The Flintstones on TV, grinning and propped up by three thick, boulder-like hospital pillows. She clicked off the set and smiled at the doctor and scanned us strangers. Then Dr. Willings gently said, "Sally, I've brought you some very special visitors. They are so glad they found you. They are here to help you."

Sally looked puzzled and said, "I don't understand," to which her doctor responded, "This young lady," pointing to Johnny, "is your sister. And this young man is her friend Thomas."

Sally thought it was some kind of joke and said, "Are you testing my memory again doctor? Are these some medical students you've got working for you now?"

"No, Sally. What I'm saying is true. This young lady really is your sister. The mystery of who you are has been solved."

"Solved," she repeated. And there was an interval of silence as if something seemed to be approaching.

"But I don't know her," she said through welling tears.

Then she turned to Johnny and said, "Please don't be insulted, I'm just so confused, I really don't know who you are," and Johnny moved to her bedside and took her hand and said, "Don't worry Sally, I've got mountains of photos and videos and family stuff to share with you. You'll remember everything as we share."

"That's correct," said her doctor, both of them knowing this was not true but had to be said to calm Sally down so the construction project could begin.

"Really?"

"Really."

Sally started to breathe regularly, and she wiped her tears and struggled to smile as she wiped them, and then it hit her that it was true, and with us all warmly looking at her she stopped crying and smiled genuinely and said, "My sister?"

And Johnny responded, "Yes, your sister. I love you, and I have been so worried."

"You love me?"

By her response it was clear that her sister was a stranger right now and that the word love was a microscopic seed that had been planted just now in the fertile but blank soil of her mind, and it was also clear that it was all starting to seem real and there was a look of hope in her eyes.

"Do you know my friend, Dave?" she asked Johnny. "He's the only friend I have. He's been so good to me."

Johnny motioned to me and said, "He's Tom's friend. They've worked together for years. It's because of Dave that we found you. I'll explain everything later."

Sitting propped there, and loosely covered in sheets, Sally turned her head and looked straight into my eyes. Her hair was pulled back in a ponytail and her cheeks still showed mild reddening from her facial abrasions, but her mouth was flawless, no swelling lips or cuts, and when she smiled not the slightest chip on any tooth, and her eyes were unbruised and still the luminous clear blue of my dreams, and with her eyes now real, no longer a memory, she looked through me like the blank window and complete stranger that I now was, and said, "It's good to meet you, 'Dave's friend,'" and smiled without showing her teeth.

"It's good to meet you too, Johnny's sister."

"But Johnny is a man's name," she said, turning suddenly to Johnny, and then to her doctor. "This *is* a test, isn't it?" And she started to tremble and look around her room in jerks.

"I know it sounds strange, Sally, but Mom and Dad really did name me Johnny. It's actually a funny story.

I'll explain everything as we spend time together," Johnny said in a cheerful and comforting tone.

Dr. Willings interjected, "Are you okay, Sally?"

"Yes, I guess so," Sally answered with a slight quiver in her voice. "As long as Johnny really is my sister."

"She really is, Sally. And she loves you and is so glad she found you."

With that confirmation, Sally relaxed back into her pillows and started to breathe in deep relaxed inhales and smiled at Johnny and said, "My sister's name is Johnny. I like her doctor. I think I'll keep her!"

And she motioned Johnny to move closer for a hug.

After Johnny hugged Sally, she said to me, "Tom, would you mind leaving us alone for a while? Just thirty minutes or so and we'll try to work out the details of Sally's discharge. All right?"

"Certainly," I said, "I'll listen to music in the truck. Text me if you want me to come back."

"I will."

"So good to meet you," I said to Sally as I slowly started to leave the room. "And thank you so much doctor. You have been incredibly helpful."

Just as I was entering the hall, I heard Sally say in a low voice, "He is *so* cute. Where did you find him?" And Johnny responded, "Shhh. I know. Actually, he found me."

When I got back to the truck it hit me that years of emotions were now gone like a blast. There was literally nothing to think about. It was all erased. I had a fresh start. And the word fresh made me think of Subway. And I flashed back to my college years and the time I saw Al Purdy read "At the Quinte Hotel" on the UBC campus, standing there with his long hair combed back and a tooth-pick hanging from his lower lip and all of us students and professors laughing, and I thought to myself, You are a sensitive man, Tom. Then I popped in "Nowhere to Run," set the volume low, and sat back and rested my eyes. I dozed off for a second and had a flash of that movie where the rich young woman is ascending the staircase in the slum apartment building with fighting and cries emanating from the walls around her, and then the passenger door of the truck opened and Johnny jumped in and said, "Sleeping like an old man, eh? We're all set. Dr. Willings says we can pick Sally up on our way to the airport tomorrow. She's good to go to New York and begin her new life."

"Airport?"

"Yes please, Tom. My flight leaves at 6:00 p.m. tomorrow from the south terminal just across town at the airport. If we leave Vermilion around noon that should be fine."

"Okay. I'll let George know he needs to fill in for me for another day."

"What's wrong?" she asked. I guess my face was easy to read.

"I'm going to miss you. You'll be gone. I just met you, and you're gone. And Sally is gone. I don't know, it's been an interesting week."

"It's not over, it's beginning, for Sally and us," she said and reached for my hand.

"We'll talk on the phone, we'll use Skype, maybe we'll even write love letters like John Keats and Fanny Brawne," she said and squeezed my hand smiling.

"Absolutely. And in the future someone will make a fortune auctioning them off," I said, forcing a grin.

"You're not going to get rid of me that easily, Tom. I really care about you."

I thought of Keats' "When I have Fears" and of his epitaph in Rome and of all of the uncertainties in my heart.

Johnny's green eyes were sincere. She explained that she couldn't promise, but there was a good chance she might be able to visit the lake a couple of times before actually moving into her house in about seven months. She said there'd be many teleconferences with the builders with a webcam that was actually already set up on a twenty-foot laminated beam set in concrete at the road edge of her lot. All of the sold lots had this security service installed as soon as construction commenced. The entire construction project would be documented. She was looking forward to watching her house rise before her very eyes through time-lapse photography. She was already auto-saving every twenty-four hour reel on her hard drive.

"Do you want to grab something to eat before we head back to the lake? Or just get going?" I asked her.

"Let's buy some French bread and deli and fruit and drinks to eat on the road," she replied.

"Sounds good," I said. I started up the truck, pulled out of the lot and before turning onto the main highway stopped at Vito's Deli. We left the music off for the first half hour or so of our drive. Then I eventually said, "It was so strange seeing Sally today. When she looked right through me without any memories at all it was like she had died."

"Part of her has died, Tom, but she's alive and has a future. Everything dies and rises, seeds push through valleys scorched by fire, plants, animals and people and their young. It's all seed, germination, death, and regeneration."

"So now it's *Leaves of Grass*, eh?" I said and cheered up.

"Yeah," Johnny replied, "I loaf and invite my soul."

We both laughed and felt more at ease as we debated what to listen to as we drove. I recommended anything by Percy Sledge, but she prevailed with Martha & the Vandellas "Heatwave," and we just sat back and cruised with the speakers pumping.

When we came to the Vermilion Lake turnoff, Johnny turned down the sound and asked me, "What was it like building this road? You said it took seven years."

"Seven years of blasting rock and heavy equipment growling."

"Tell me about it."

So I gave her the skeletal details of how my work days were structured and how the natural geography was shaken and transformed by us, but she sensed that my objective description was sterile.

"Since when did your life become a dry documentary?"

"What do you mean?"

"That isn't the real story, is it Tom?"

"What do you mean by real story?"

"That description sounds like an engineering report or something. Where's the myth? The symbols? What's up?"

"You'll laugh, but maybe also be hurt if I tell you the whole thing?"

"The whole thing about everything is mandatory from now on. Is that a deal?" she asked me and I nodded.

"Mom always told us girls that 'one hundred percent communication combined with intimacy levels right through the roof' were the necessary combination for a happy marriage. Those were her exact words, and she and Dad were happy. So tell me the truth," she said and winked, "handsome."

"Okay, here goes. Throughout the whole project, I always thought of the time Sally and I had together when we were young. I was a blaster's helper and twice a day for seven years, excluding Sundays, we detonated massive charges of dynamite to blow a path for this road."

As I narrated, I pointed to odd-looking ridges of boulders and plant patterns on new rolling hills of stones that our work had created.

"After the Subway scene today I really don't know what it is with you sisters, but the way Sally kissed me all those years ago was mythic. Everything about her face and eyes and especially her mouth was perfect. From an evolutionary perspective, I guess some might say that our kissing was a transitory beauty which could never endure in the real world. But it did in my mind. While we were blasting, with every one of those explosions, just before the charges blew, I'd see her blue eyes, her long gently curled black hair, her flawless skin. Before every blast, I thought of her perfect mouth. It was a good memory to detonate twice a day for seven years. And every night of those seven years, there alone in my tent on the edge of camp, as I shut my eyes to sleep, like a rhythmic ritual I thought of Sally and wondered if she ever thought of me. I could see her for a moment, and then everything would dissolve. Like in the hospital this morning."

I looked over at Johnny to see her reaction because she had been listening in complete silence, and her face was turned away from me and looking at the passing scenery and she was wiping tears away. I waited a minute or so, then asked, "Are you okay? You wanted the truth and that is it."

I could see that she was deeply moved, and I didn't want to rush her, so I drove on in silence. Then she turned to me, "Tom, you're the most beautiful man I've ever met. Let's pull over and have some lunch. We need to keep up our strength. And I want to kiss you again right now. Okay?"

Totally relieved, I smiled and said, "Okay," and then in about three minutes pulled over at the first rest area we came to. It was around 3:30 p.m. As soon as the ignition was off, Johnny unbuckled her seatbelt and got up on the bench seat and knelt next to me and smiling widely with wet tear stains still on her cheeks said, "Let's blast some rock!" and kissed me. The tires didn't blow off the truck, there was no pinkish-blue mushroom cloud in the distance, no massive explosion and granite shower, just her natural fragrance, her unbelievable form in my arms, strands of her hair against my face, and her heart beating close to mine. We kissed there in the company pickup for several minutes. We were falling in love on the road to Vermilion Lake.

We ate our lunch at one of the picnic tables looking out over miles of rolling dry hills and boulder ridges. Countless cacti and small blooming plants were scattered throughout the shady pockets along the ridges, and there was a verdant artery thick with salal and black huckleberry shrubs along both sides of Windhover Creek, which cold and clear wound its way through the hills, down from Vermilion Lake in the far distance above us and out of sight behind the mountains on the horizon. Once we got back into the truck and onto the road, Johnny talked to me about Easter.

"Love cannot be destroyed, Tom. He literally rose from the dead."

I hadn't expected that. And when she was finished there was a pause, and I said respectfully, "Do you believe those things, exactly as you've explained them to me just now?"

And she said, "Yes I do, Tom. As we're driving can I play a CD that Dad loved?"

"Motown?"

"No, this one is Gregorian chant, compositions from the eighth century. I know it's medieval, but give it a chance. It's the Easter Mass sung by the monks at Fontgombault Abbey. For a few minutes at least, okay?"

"Sure. Go for it."

I'd heard the phone music at the convents I'd contacted, but this was a full Mass. The higher sound quality and coherence and structure surprised me. The music sounded extremely otherworldly but also extremely grounded at the same time, as if the men singing it were both calloused-hands farmers and scholarly contemplatives, which it turns out they were.

After a couple of pieces, Johnny turned it down and asked, "Enough?"

But I said, "No. Let it play. It's different."

As we drove, I absorbed the scenery as a tourist might with one eye, and with the other eye like a builder who sweated along each mile of this road. And with the chant as our soundtrack, the entire valley seemed like a natural cathedral. Eventually the CD ended and Johnny ejected it and put it carefully back into its case and into her backpack and said, "That was Dad's favorite. He claimed it went well with Motown, and it contrasted with the roaring of the funny cars he loved so much. It was part of his version of the modern Renaissance man, I guess."

"A unique combination," I said. "It would have been so cool to have known your dad."

"I'll never forget him, Tom," she said and smiled without sadness.

"We were so close. It's strange, but sometimes I dream about the day he died in the explosion."

Johnny moved herself firmly back into her seat and adjusted her seatbelt so that she was snuggly secure and continued: "In my dream there are engine parts scattered all over the pavement, and everywhere burning oil and black smoke, and then a fresh gush of wind blows hard across the scene and I see him standing up—pushing scorched fuel lines and timing chains from his shoulders, and then he pulls a rag out of his coverall pocket and wipes the soot and grease from his face and smiles at me and says my name. And then I wake up, and in the quiet of the night I sense that he's still alive somewhere, and it feels like I could just get up and drive there to wherever he is and visit him. But then I remember the exploding engine, and my mind shifts gears into heaven."

"Heaven?" I repeated.

"Yes, heaven."

It was around 6:00 p.m. when we arrived at Vermilion Lake, and we had a few hours before sunset. The lake looked beautiful, like a pinkish mirror reflecting the few clouds above it, and the air was cool and fresh. Johnny looked tired, but she asked me if I'd like to visit her lot while there was still light. She wanted to explain her plans and walk me around the property so I could visualize her dream house. I said sure, and she directed me through the streets to her place.

I was stunned. What a contrast to my company trailer pad. It was a beautiful 1.5 acre lot right on the lakeshore. She said, "My hope is that after a month or so in New York with Sally we will be able to settle the issue of whether or not she wants to permanently live with me or strike out on her own. Part of the answer will be based on her reaction to my reconstruction of her past, and part based on her physical recovery, whether or not it is complete and she is one hundred percent again."

She went on, "My current blueprints could easily be adjusted into a duplex design if necessary once Sally has made her decision."

On her phone she showed me pictures of her floor plan, and she excitedly talked about some of the high quality building materials they were planning to use, yellow cedar logs, black marble, and so on. As she guided me towards the shore and began explaining her plans for what sounded like an extraordinary clear Plexiglas patio deck which she hoped to extend right out into the water—freshwater plants, fry, and innumerable shoreline organisms thriving beneath it in full view from above—I suppose my face looked drained and my inner misgivings were evident because she asked, "What's wrong, Tom?"

I thought about my answer carefully, and then said, "Johnny, your plans sound incredible, but I'm starting to wake up."

"What do you mean, wake up?"

"Don't you think we are a mismatch? I've got three years of college. I'm a construction worker with less than $15,000 in savings. You're an environmental architect with an advanced degree and a high salary. This land and house, I can't even imagine the cost. I'm feeling so out of my league here. I'm starting to have an old-school provider crisis, if you know what I mean? You just seem so above me."

"I understand your feelings, Tom, but I'm not rich. Believe me. This place will have a thirty-year mortgage. I might die of old age before it's paid off. Wealth is peace of mind, number one, and health of body, number two, and both simultaneously, number three."

Then she smirked at her own parallel construction which seemed awkward and not particularly climactic.

"My dad and mom once sat us down and said to us girls that if ever something happened to one of us, something really serious like a terrible sickness or being kidnapped or something horrible like that, they would happily sell everything they had and empty every bank account and even take off their clothes and include them in the payment for whatever it cost to heal or get back safely one of us girls. I remember Dad standing up and saying loudly, 'Whatever the cost!' And Mom saying, 'Don't frighten them, Roman, please sit down.' And they said that when that girl was safely well or back and we were all standing naked and penniless in the street with nothing, we would praise God that we had each other and then get to work starting all over and find some way to live again, to buy clothes and food and whatever. Health and family, Tom, that's wealth."

"Visualizing you all together naked is a bit awkward, but I get it. That's a grounded view."

"And while we're talking about money, I've decided that I will include in the revised lake development plans the three 1000 yard shooting ranges you suggested. Will New thought it was a great idea, and he told me that the best shooters at the highest level in international contests can win annual prize money in the $200,000 to $1,000,000 range. Will says target shooting has become as rewarding as professional golf. How would that kind of money ease your male ego there, Mr. Tems?"

She grinned and went on, "All you would have to do is practice and become the best, and in your spare time have candlelight dinners with me on my patio overlooking the lake. Sound endurable?"

"Very endurable. What do you say I drive you back to your motel?"

"Absolutely."

It was now just after 9:00 p.m. and dark. And once I got her back to Gold Motel we kissed just inside the door of her motel room, and then we agreed that I'd pick her up at noon to head for the hospital to get Sally. We'd then go to the airport and they'd be away to New York. Then I'd return to my first-aid station and Dave would share his broken heart with me once Sally was gone. Sally and Dave had agreed to phone and use Skype, just like Johnny and I were going to do. Dave had apparently told Sally that she seemed to be linked to his destiny. She had responded by saying that time would tell.

I left Johnny's room after a few minutes and another kiss, and then heard her lock click, and drove back to my trailer to shower and sleep.

CHAPTER NINE:

Once I fell asleep, I saw the woman ascending the stairs in the slum apartment, but this time the building was simple, clean, and freshly painted, and there were no screams or howls. A well-dressed woman in her fifties with a shopping bag passed the young lady in the hall and after answering her query, directed her to her lover's apartment, number 59 at the end of the hall. Then my mind shifted to fishing with Dad on the Okanagan River and to the unbelievable hunger of the steelhead there in the rushing cold river and sparkling sun and heat. Then blank and my alarm went off.

    I packed us a lunch for the trip, and then figured I should drop by my first-aid station to check in with George before picking Johnny up to head back to the hospital and airport. I had the day off, but I didn't like to leave my station for long. Anytime I did, supplies seemed to go missing or be misplaced or something, and when someone is bleeding all over your floor there's no time to start looking for what you need. George was there, and he was surprised to see me.

    "What's up," he said, "I thought you wanted me to take your shift today?"

    "I do. I just thought I'd check in before picking up Johnny."

George grinned and said, "How's it going with her?"

"This woman is classic, George. In a league by herself. Hard to understand."

"Good luck with that, Tom. Maybe this is your time to shine, eh?"

"Maybe," I said. "Yesterday go okay?"

"It was a strange day. Late in the afternoon there was a tremor on the east side of the lake. It caused a rockslide and two cement workers had to bolt out of there to escape the shower of rock that came down."

"What the hell?"

"Yeah. They could easily have been pinned under heaps of sharp-edged stones. Later the same day around nightfall there was another minor tremor, but no rock came down that time."

"What did Will New say?"

"He said there were no seismic issues reported when they first researched the area before surveying and planning the development. He's not sure what to make of it, but said they'll be checking it out now and monitoring the ground."

George laughed and then joked, "Maybe Vermilion Lake is a dormant volcano—maybe we're building on a powder keg—and maybe the beauty of the area and the potential for profit prevented the original real estate entrepreneurs from even considering this possibility?"

"Or maybe all is well, and it was just a freak blip in geological time? Millions of years and here we are for a few and then gone. Blips of beauty, blips of rock, right?" I said, trying to be witty and profound simultaneously.

"I'll give that some thought while you're enjoying Johnny's company today, Tom," he said with a smile. "Make the day count."

And I replied, "That's deep, seriously. I'll do my best."

And then I checked that George had all of the supplies he needed and said I'd be back on the job at 8:00 a.m. the next day and he could plan on returning to his framing crew on the east side of the lake.

As I pulled into the motel parking lot, I let George's advice echo in my mind, "Make the day count." He was right. Johnny and I had just connected and she was soon to leave. I don't care what movies, stories, love letters, or anything else say about the matter, the fact is when your partner in love is out of sight and smell and taste and touch, your nervous system feels the vacuum no matter how hard the memory tries to fill it, and I resolved to make our last day together count.

I knocked on Johnny's door and she opened it immediately. She was ready to go and had three large suitcases packed and ready for me to toss into the box of the truck. She was wearing just a slight trace of makeup and her green eyes were largish and naturally stunning, and the way she looked at me showed a deep reservoir of hope for us, a look billions of times removed from an airbrushed mask in some fashion magazine. She was wearing a white summer dress, with a soft orange and pale yellow pattern. She had that incredible medieval way of being a modern damsel not in any sense in distress but rather in bold presence. She might use the word freak, but for me "of great worth" seemed to fit better. Her glossy red hair shone in the noon sun and she had it loose and down and lifted back over her shoulders, unfettered except for emerald hair brooches holding the strands at each temple to keep her hair out of her eyes.

She saw me take her in from top to bottom and return to her eyes and silently look into them, and then she said, "Hi, Tom. Do I look okay?"

"You look as beautiful as a woman can look, Johnny. You are a miracle."

"A miracle? So I've already got you doing theology, eh?" she said and smiled.

"Yes. But I suddenly feel so underdressed."

"Nonsense. I can gaze too. Let me barcode you. You look great in your clean faded jeans and fresh white T-shirt and sandals, nice and freshly showered and a bit stubbly because you were probably too busy tossing and turning and not able to sleep thinking about how today is our last day together. You eventually passed out and then had no time to shave, right?"

I playfully smirked at her catalogue and answered with a partial truth, "Actually, I dreamt about fishing for steelhead with my dad when I was a boy."

Johnny sparked back, "I'll never forget how Mom took me to the river every winter until I caught my first steelhead. When that 27 ½ inch wild hen hit my Gibbs-Delta CROC copper fire wing spoon, it was like a hand grenade exploding in the tailout."

"You are unreal."

"We'll fish together in the winter," she said, and then kissed me with a tender firmness on the mouth.

"Sounds good. Shall we drive?"

"Yes. Let's get Sally, then fly," she said and motioned as if gently doing the breaststroke into the sky above us.

Once we got into the truck, I pressed on the radio and Johnny turned down the volume and said, "Something special, Tom," and pulled out of her handbag a CD by Percy Sledge. It was his greatest hits.

"I'd like to make this day count, Tom."

"Count?" I said surprised.

"Yeah. We both need to really get to know each other."

"But how does that link to Percy Sledge?"

"Listen to 'Take time to know her' and 'When a man loves a woman' as we drive, okay?"

"Pop it in and let's ride." And she did.

As we drove, I listened carefully to the lyrics and Percy's heartfelt emotions and when the CD finished I said to her, "Those are sincere and beautiful songs, but I don't see you in them. You are entirely different."

"Maybe so, Tom, but you need to know that difference from experience. We need to take time. Okay?"

"Time to know you, and me," I said.

"Yeah."

When we pulled into the hospital parking lot I was surprised to see another company truck there and I hoped no one had gotten hurt on the job that morning. Sally had texted Johnny that she was out of her room, packed and ready to be picked up at the main entrance waiting area. When we walked through the sliding doors, Dr. Willings was there with her, and so was Dave. I didn't expect to see him, but I guess it made sense that Sally would contact him about her leaving. Dave had taken the day off too and was dressed in a suit he'd worn to a friend's wedding a few years ago. I'd never seen him dressed up and he looked good. Sally had that glow a woman has when she's next to a man she's really into, and with her black hair up in a messy bun and her blue eyes matching her blue blouse and her tight white jeans and her white sandals, she looked really good next to Dave in his charcoal suit and ultra-pale yellow dress shirt without a tie and his trimmed neat blonde beard and combed back longish blonde hair atop his well-built 5' 11" frame. They were a nice looking couple, I had to admit, but she was Johnny's sister and I was protective and suspicious given Dave's track record with women in the bar scene. I couldn't recall a single woman he'd met at Mass, let's put it that way, and Sally was one of that crowd, however blown her memories of God might have been.

Sally stood up very happy to see us and gave Johnny a big hug, "Hey, sis. To New York and away!" she said and grinned.

"Yeah. In ninety minutes we'll be in the sky soaring over Vermilion Lake and then up and to the Big Apple. If the sky is clear, I'll show you my design for the lake."

"Your design?"

"I'll explain in the air."

Dave drove to the airport with Sally while Johnny rode with me. At the airport we sat at a distance in pairs and tried to savor the few minutes we had left. When the announcer's voice eventually called for the passengers to board, we'd have to let go. Across from us, I could see Dave in a posture that I'd not seen him in before. It seemed to indicate a kind of sincerity of speech. But I didn't watch him and Sally for more than a few seconds. I was focusing on Johnny.

"This is it," she said. "The beginning for us."

"Yeah. The beginning."

And then we stood up together. She hugged me gently then pulled back and gave me a serious tender look then held me close again. Her breasts were against my chest, and she looked up into my eyes with her green eyes and said, "You are a special man, Tom

Tems," and then she kissed me very slowly and then a bit more wetly and then pulled back and snuggled in again so that I felt the slow rush of her breasts leaving my body and then returning to my body and pressing softly there.

All of the lonely nights and blown rock and bloody injuries of the last eight years flashed through my mind.

Then her lips made a barely audible wet leaving sound, a delicious sticky sound, and returned firm and barely touching and wetter and then fully touching and then softly pulled back.

And then she said, "Walk me down to the boarding tunnel, Tom, please," and I said, "Of course, let's make every minute count."

As she gave me a final kiss, she whispered mysteriously into my ear, "I'll be with you, Tom."

It was clear that Sally would now be her main construction project. Johnny would have to somehow balance Sally and work in New York, with me on the other side of the continent far in the distant mountains of Vermilion Lake. It had been an incredible surprise meeting her, not at all like the routine blood test that I tried to make it.

Dave and Sally kissed and then pulled apart too, but before Sally joined Johnny to finally leave, she walked over and gave me a big hug and said, "This is like a scene in a movie, isn't it, Tom?"

"Absolutely," I answered.

Then Johnny looked at me warmly and pulled me close and said, "I will be praying for us, Tom."

And then she kissed my cheek and walked down the tunnel with Sally. After a few quick backward glances and mutual waves they turned right and vanished.

Dave and I stood there motionless in silence for a couple of minutes, and then Dave looked at me and said deeply and firmly, "Son of a bitch."

And I said, "You got that right."

We walked up to the departure viewing area and sat in silence as their plane took to the runway, then accelerated, and then lifted off into the blank blue sky. I remember the sky was the exact color of Sally's eyes, not similar, but exact.

CHAPTER TEN:

After they disappeared, Dave and I got a coffee and some pie in the airport cafeteria.

"I'm missing her already," Dave said.

"She's an excellent woman," I replied.

"You guys will stay in touch, I assume. Did you talk to Sally about that?"

"Yeah, we'll use Skype, text, the usual. But I don't know about this other side of the continent plan. I've got needs. Needs."

Our young waitress brought our coffees and pies, mine was peach, Dave's was blueberry, and after smiling at us both she walked away with her white apron bow tied in back. She was healthy looking, and we both watched her walk away from us.

Dave said, "Nature."

And I responded, "Natural law," which was a new concept I'd learned from Johnny.

"Think of the future, and talk to Sally about your needs. Be honest."

"No man thinks about the future when he's got a hard-on. Wood blinds a man. And honest? It's never occurred to me to be honest with women. Honesty equals disaster."

"If it doesn't work, it doesn't work, but I'd give it a shot. Sally seems incredible. I know her sister is. I think she might be my destiny. Didn't you tell Sally she was linked to your destiny?"

"I used the word, yeah. But what the fuck is destiny, really? I don't know. Maybe tragedy, more pain?"

"Not tragedy, happiness."

"Happiness? How does reality fit in with happiness, Tom? We're not little boys and girls."

"St. Thomas Aquinas writes that nearly all human actions, no matter how warped or dysfunctional, are motivated by the desire for happiness. I read that in a book Johnny gave me."

"Saint? Are you shitting me? Has she got you into some kind of take religion seriously cult or something?"

"Not a cult, something medieval. She's into the whole time period and the ethos is actually kind of interesting."

"You mean like damsels in towers wearing chastity belts and monks with chicks on the side or lashing the hell out of their backs to help them forget about Rosie?"

And Dave continued, "Careful where you go man. The bars are air-conditioned, the strippers are red hot and love to show us all they have—no mystery, the beer is ice cold, and there are chicks swarming the clubs looking for love, the kind of love that is free and fast and without chains."

This was the pre-Sally Dave I'd always known, talking now.

"No chains? You sure about that?"

"Yes I am, no chains."

"So how does Sally fit in? Is she chaining you? Or setting you free?"

"She's different, man, but she's gone now and I'm not sure how long we'll last apart. She didn't leave me any saints books to read. She only left me her kisses, and I know kissing sounds stupid in our 'do me completely and by the way what's your name, no don't bother answering, it doesn't matter,' scene, man."

"Her kisses?"

"Yeah. I've done more chicks than I can remember, Tom, and I regret nothing. It was all hot sex and I've been lucky and I'm still not sick. Then along comes Sally. Sally gave me no body heat at all, couldn't get to first base with her, not even a bunt. Damn. I've never heard any woman in the twenty-first century use the word chaste in a sentence."

Our waitress passed our table and asked if everything was fine, and we both nodded and asked to have our coffees topped up. As she poured, her arms were obviously neither skinny nor soft and thick, but rather, were moderately muscular like a female athlete's arms, and her pale yellow dress uniform snugged against her ribs and showed a lean torso.

Dave continued as the waitress moved away, "I had to ask her what the hell the word meant, exactly. And when she told me I laughed aloud. She teared up as I was laughing and I shut up. Something about her tears stopped me in my tracks."

He was restless and adjusted his posture, arching his shoulders back against his tension.

"And as I got to know her during my visits, I felt a change I can't describe because I don't know what the hell it is really. Part of me looked at her beautiful face and body and just wanted to epic bang her right there and then and make her moan, but that same face and body was saying to me, 'we need a higher love.' You know the song?"

"Steve Winwood is good," I said. "I got the same physical vibe and higher love vibe from Johnny. I guess we'll both see how it goes, eh?"

"Yeah, how it goes."

I could see that during the upcoming months Dave and I would be getting to know each other better. But I also knew that if Dave ever disrespected Sally and treated her like a piece of tail (his frequently used expression, not mine), that we'd become instant strangers. Even though I was as transparent to Sally as the plate glass in a prison visiting area, my memories of her were rock solid.

Dave and I finished our coffees and drove back to the lake in our company trucks to get ready for work the next day. Dave's trailer was a block over from mine, and I was glad to see he went home and not to the bar as he usually did. The next day I was back on the job at 8:00 a.m. and I reviewed George's records for the previous days. There were no serious accidents beyond the injuries he previously described to me in person. As I was checking supplies, the phone rang and Will New told me, "There was another tremor after work yesterday around 6:00 p.m. It was a bitch that brought tons of rock down into the lower sites on the east side and covered three foundations that were ready to frame." He was pissed off and said they were shutting down the entire east side until the ground could be fully assessed. "The situation is fucking ridiculous. No one can work safely there. I'm just glad as hell that no one got hurt," he said. And I agreed.

Soon after Will hung up, my cell tone rang and I was happy to see a text coming in from Johnny: "Dear Mr. Keats. Safely landed in NY. So busy with work and Sally. I will write you an old-school letter as soon as time allows. From my heart, Fanny."

I said aloud, "She was serious. So now our mailboxes have become Grecian urns decorated with nightingales?"

I texted her back: "I'll try to get an inkwell, pen, and wax signet ring. So glad you are safe. From my heart, J.K." And I thought again of Keats' epitaph in Rome.

Obviously, the vacation was over for Johnny, and she was already swamped with work, constructing Sally's past, and taking her to her checkups and sessions. Writing would be good. It would give us both some time to think and breathe, and I laughed at the thought that this Percy Sledge-like plan to take time to know her was coming from a knockout who mentioned marriage within the first twenty-four hours of meeting me. A medieval ethos at funny car record speed, I thought to myself and chuckled. I'd wait for her first letter, and then write back.

That day at work stayed quiet. The tremors had stopped and the rest of the work week was thankfully quiet too, just a few of the inevitable small cuts and plywood splinters in the eyes. As I checked supplies and tried to look busy, I thought about the years that I'd worked with Dave. I'd always known that he had gone to art school. As we blasted our way into Vermilion Lake he had mentioned how at times he had been tempted to draw some of the women he had banged over the years, but he had said to himself, "What's the point?" But it wasn't until later the following week that one afternoon he opened up to me and shared what art had meant and still meant to him.

He came in around eleven on a Thursday. We were alone and had lots of time to talk while I was rebandaging his hand. The swelling was down and it was healing well. A few more days and the bandage could stay off to let the air at the wound for final healing. He knew I liked to read, and I mentioned that I had just finished reading a novel Johnny had given me before leaving. It was a story about a tattoo artist who fell insanely in love with a woman he had tattooed over three years. In the novel, she commissions him to create a body suit design using her personal themes and symbols, which takes him about three months of sketching, discussion, and revision. Then she commissions him to apply the design to her body. She has money and asks for extreme details: numerous colors, exact shading, chiaroscuro effects, the whole deal, and she knows there will be a huge cost and time commitment. The tattooist guesses it will take approximately two hundred hours to complete the suit, but that might change depending on her reaction to the inks and the pain. She is religious, he is not, and the design incorporates the four seasons and images of embryos in utero, childhood, youth, adulthood, and onwards until the figures are entering caves much like William Blake portrays old age in his later engravings, and the suit also includes set-pieces illustrating the resurrection of the dead with Michael and other holy angels acting as guides for the countless dead throughout the ages.

When I got to this point in my plot summary, Dave interjected with "Damn," and I agreed that the story was heavy duty.

I continued to explain that the design is ambitious and the artist has to be a modern master, and he is. As he works for years on her in private sessions, she opens herself to him as if his studio has the divine security of a confessional, and as she shares her ecstasies and horrors he comes to know her soul and her flesh intimately and he falls utterly in love with her.

It took me about half an hour to enthusiastically share Johnny's book with Dave, and his attention was riveted. When I had finished, he responded to the novel's ending by saying emphatically, "Damn," and I said, "Yeah. Damn."

"That's wild, man. Johnny gave you that book?"
"She did."

Alluding to some of the female character's horrors in the novel, Dave explained that although he was educated in the arts, he "fell down a mine shaft" when he was young.

"I ended up smashed at the bottom of a dark hole somewhere. I fought it like hell, but I still ended up doing Federal time. Over-fucking-whelmed."

This genuinely surprised me because Dave didn't at all have a convict aura about him. He said that in the penitentiary he was surrounded by things he didn't want to discuss with me. When I asked him, "How bad was it?" He replied, "My best friend in the joint, Miles, went fucking nuts. He wanted out so bad he broke a razor blade into tiny slivers and then rolled them up in a ball of wet toilet paper and swallowed it, and when the paper dissolved in his gut the fragments sliced him up from the inside. He started puking blood and had to be rushed to an emergency unit out in the world."

"That bad?" I said.

"Oh yeah. And when they brought him back all stitched up in a week, he requested solitary and they said yes as they often do in cases of mental collapse, and I never saw him again. As far as I know he did the rest of his bit alone in the hole with nothing but a few blankets and a Bible."

"Unreal," I said.

"Fucking real," Dave responded. "Art saved me. I started sketching as soon as the police gave me sheets of paper in lockup, and by the time I got to trial and found myself on the bus to the BC Pen, I was known in the Lower Mainland corrections system as *Hell Man*. With hardly any practice I found I could draw skulls and flames superbly."

He paused and looked around my first-aid station to verify we were alone.

"Even though I never actually tattooed the inmates I lived with, they thought of me as the man. I created the best outlines for the prison tattooists to work with, and this gave me a status that acted like a shield which held back the evil that surrounded me in that cage-riddled inferno," he said.

Cage-riddled inferno, I thought to myself, and Miles in a solitary cell with a Bible.

I probed Dave gently about how he got sent to jail in the first place, and he finally shared that he had become a heroin addict at a young age.

"Just one taste and I was wired," he said. "I shot up at Stanley's place, and when I slid the needle out of my vein, sucked pinkish water into the syringe, laid it on his cluttered night table and relaxed my weight into the filthy, heavy, yellow-padded armchair, there under the dusty cross-shaped basement window by the bloody-water-stained wall forming a barrier between me and the bright white sun outside, the dope slowly penetrated my nerves and brain and within thirty seconds I was in a rainy black night filled with loud wind and I heard the crashing of metal and shattering of glass. And then I rose and staggered out the basement door and into the yard and puked my guts out and dry heaved in the sun. After I caught my breath, I wiped the puke off of my face with my T-shirt sleeve and shakily walked back in and to the chair and sank down again.

"And as the nod came fully on I slowly reached to my gold medallion of Christ—a childhood gift from my father's sister in Italy—and my thumb sensed the Italian script engraved on its back, and I moved into a state of unbelievable peace and whispered, 'Thank You.' I felt like Jesus raised from the dead, not by the Spirit of God, but by a flower.

"There was an Andrés Segovia CD spinning in the player and I was released into the sounds—notes softly together in my blood like white stars floating and scorching swirling viruses, gently connecting and echoing and webbing veins into mosaics of black and purple marble fragments. Then my bones became a cathedral—cool stone gracefully honed. Then warm black. Then nothingness."

"One taste?"

"Yeah," Dave replied. "The world had little to offer compared to that first hit. Women and booze were a joke when set alongside the pleasure of heroin in the blood. It became my religion. The only downside was that it was so fucking illegal."

Dave shared stories about the designs he had created and their owners, but one owner really stuck with me. He described him as a man in his mid-forties when he first met him in prison. He was tall and muscular and had a shaved head and a long neatly trimmed goatee. He had a kind, weathered face that showed years of spiritual struggle and intense blue eyes.

"But he wasn't to be fucked with," Dave said. "Anyone who tried to fuck with him quickly learned to back the fuck off and do his own time. His nickname was THE FATHER. He was a mechanic who was doing 20 years for murdering four men, shot each of them five times in the face at point blank range—wasted two full magazines of 45 ACP on the bastards."

The story went that these four guys were pornographers who had kidnapped his two daughters and then used them repeatedly in bondage and vicious facial abuse videos. THE FATHER said, "The sons of bitches put my girls through hell. They kept them in cages for three weeks. Cages! Christ almighty!"

Dave described how THE FATHER eventually rescued his daughters. With a stack of cash and some street research, he confirmed the identity of the four guys. Then he hunted them down and shot each one dead. He "blew their fucking heads off." It was premeditated first-degree murder. Then he turned himself in and confessed. The detectives told him in private and off the record that they had to do their job and charge him, he had committed murder, but to be honest it was good he had found the "soulless bastards" when he did because usually in similar cases the girls would "end up snuffed on camera within a month of kidnapping." Dave said he got to know him well over a two-year period, and he designed his best pieces for THE FATHER.

He created two full-sleeve designs, one dedicated to each daughter. THE FATHER's left arm was composed of brilliant green flowers and skulls and winding wreathes and jumping fish and religious symbols and passages of scripture, and his right arm was composed of brilliant blue flowers and skulls and winding wreathes and leaping bucks and religious symbols and passages of scripture. Each arm was parallel in design, but unique in its coloration and texts. All of the scripture verses spoke of saving and rescuing and purity, and all of the plants were biblical symbols. Each sleeve included seven skulls to indicate the perfect state of hell that his daughters had been rescued from, and on the inside of his left wrist was the Sacred Heart of Jesus, perfectly rendered, and on the inside of his right wrist was the Immaculate Heart of Mary, perfectly rendered. Dave said it took him three months to complete the research and outlines, and then a tattooist on their tier (whose name was *the god*) worked with Dave's designs. It was THE FATHER's sleeves that immortalized both Dave (aka *Hell Man*) and *the god* in jail, and even after Dave was released on parole after serving two years and a day, he continued to receive letters from inmates requesting tattoo commissions.

Even now, long since off parole and a free man, Dave was still creating a few designs a year. He said the living room walls of the new trailer the company had just shifted him into were covered with corkboards with various sketches pinned there. Cons' family members or friends on the outside were paying him for his work and then bringing his designs during visiting hours to their family members or friends doing time. Some prisons even had professional tattoo shops inside their institutions to cut down on the disease rates, and many of these shops had Dave's custom designs on their walls as ideal samples of his prison legacy.

The day I removed Dave's bandage for good, he shared some theories of design and discussed primitive tattoo techniques, but his earlier story of THE FATHER stood out in my memory. That father's life seemed to be a strange tangle of beauty and evil and goodness, like the life of the fictional woman with the body suit in the novel Johnny had left with me. It was mysterious and fascinating that Johnny would imagine that long process of shared designing and shared intimate pain as a fitting metaphor for our germinating love, but obviously that's the way she saw it. It was one more thing to appreciate about her. It fueled my desire to take the time to know her.

CHAPTER ELEVEN:

Exactly two weeks after Johnny left, I received her first letter. Every night we had texted each other with simple phrases like "thinking deeply about you," and so forth, but now I had something substantial in hand and was eager to read her words. The envelope was thick—almost antique-looking paper—and true to her promise, my name and address were written with pen and ink. I opened the envelope with a clean dinner knife to get a smooth tear, as obviously the letter was the first of a valuable collection. I slid the three thick folded pages out of the envelope and opened them at my well-lit desk. The handwriting was beautiful and must have taken Johnny hours. It was a labor of love. I was excited and made a fresh coffee to drink while I read.

June 9, 2014
Dear Tom:

Business before pleasure. I've incorporated your shooting range suggestions into my large schematics for the north end of the lake development. My supervisor forwarded them to the Swiss shooting federation, and they approved them with a minor revision: they must be 1000 meters, not yards, apparently, for international competitions. Will New now has the finalized plans and within two weeks the heavy equipment and surveyors will begin the installation. First, trees will have to be removed; second, heavy machinery will be employed to level and fill as required for the range pathways; then dump trucks will bring in the fine sand needed to create all of the match-sanctioned berms and safety barriers; and finally, construction crews for concrete, framing, and finishing will be brought in to complete the clubhouses and two hundred guest residences to hold the shooters who visit the lake during international competitions. Will New is very excited about the project. He feels it will boost Vermilion's international status in Europe as an elite real estate investment. He estimates that the ranges will be completed and open for use within five months. And I really want to thank you for your suggestion Tom, because I certainly would never have thought of it. Once the ranges are ready, you can begin practicing for the professional circuit.

That's the business part, now comes the Sally update part. I'll conclude with the pleasure part.

I paused and smiled at Johnny's love of order. There would be no chaotic rambling from her. I knew that whatever Johnny's Catholic upbringing and education would ultimately and eventually mean to me, it seemed clear already that it somehow tried to balance the rational and the emotional, the mind and the body, the scientific and the mystical, and somehow marriage seemed to be a nucleus of sorts, what she called "a big deal" when describing her childhood and youth. I topped up my coffee and continued reading.

Sally has occasionally mentioned you and referred to you as cute, but certainly no memories have returned. Her memories of Dave seem to be fragmented and fading. It's as if they didn't get a chance to really fix themselves in her mind (the doctor told me the technical term for this, but I forget it), and Dave hasn't answered any of her earlier texts. If you can discreetly ask Dave if his phone is working, first of all, and then maybe if he's heard from Sally, and then get back to me, that would be great. If it's meant to be that Dave fades out of her life, that's fine with me because he's so far away and she's got so much healing ahead of her and a new life to embrace here on the East Coast. I've been reminding her of the main events of her life daily, usually for about an hour every night, and of course you are never mentioned. She absorbs my narratives without resistance, but the most awkward part is our Catholic upbringing. She's like a child who has never heard the word God before, and I'm really struggling because so much of what we learned as kids was through subtly absorbing everything around us. I took her to Mass last week and found myself overwhelmed with questions about literally everything said and done during the service. It is surreal to think she was on the verge of a tour of convents in Quebec when the accident at the lake happened. It's a daily trial, but also a chance for me to grow because I'm realizing now just how mysterious our faith must seem to outsiders. It's so strange to have 'medieval Sally,' a Notre Dame Drama major, in my impromptu beginner's catechism class. I can only trust that God has a plan in this for me and her.

And now for the pleasure part, Mr. Tems.

When our flight lifted off, I looked down at the airport terminal and thought of you there. With each second the plane was lifting me further away from you. I looked over at Sally and smiled and made a few comments about the beauty *of the sky and landscape, but the landscape of my soul was emptying. I don't know if you're familiar with Emily Carr's writings, but she describes the life force in nature as a kind of primal fluid energy, a life juice that surges upwards through the trees and every living thing. As the plane ascended and the airport became a speck and then vanished like a grain of sand on the horizon, I could literally feel the juice and strength of life draining out of me. I guess you could say that I like you a lot Thomas Neal Tems. Work has been helpful; I'm immersed in plans and project details and permits and bureaucracy daily, and it fills my time, but as soon as I leave the office and my mind has moments of freedom, my soul immediately returns to you. I think of how you looked at me every time we met, how you respected me in spite of what probably seemed or still seems to be my medieval—in the pejorative sense—spirituality, the way I felt so incredibly feminine next to you and how you made me and make me want to be all I can possibly be as a woman, your open mind, your rugged looks but gentle heart, and your willingness to wait and make what we've begun special and different. I think of how you kissed me and let me kiss you and the beautiful tenderness but deep passion I felt there like a force only marriage could contain, and how you didn't flinch when I mentioned marriage, Tom, that meant so much to me and said so much about what kind of man you are. I've really missed you, and I've been struggling in your absence, but my hope for us has also been growing, and I can feel it and imagine it building slowly and purely towards a climax.*

Also, and this is really important, since I've met you I've been feeling very awkward about my lot at the lake and the design I have for my house. We discussed how it could be adjusted to accommodate Sally if that would be good for her, but that still seems to leave you as an outsider looking on. I've decided to leave my property at the lake as it is. The water, sewer, and electricity have all been brought in, but the concrete foundation has not been poured yet. It's like a blank canvas, and I'm just going to leave it at that for now, on hiatus, and give our relationship a chance to grow without my dream house being the backdrop for all of our discussions and decisions. If things go well for us, then we'll plan it as our dream house, not mine. And I hope, if things go well, that you'll agree that our dream house should contain many rooms for children. And if things go well and we decide to not live at the lake, we can sell the lot and build our future wherever we want. My lot is not an idol to me. I hope this sounds good to you. I feel fresher and happier now that I've halted the building.

Finally, until my next letter, please know that I think about your physical presence every night as I fall asleep. It's as if you're there in the bed next to me, your eyes and lips and hands and the full length of your body warming me, almost touching, almost kissing. Let me be close to you as you fall asleep too, every night. There in your warm bed, there for you alone.

God bless you, Tom

Johnny

I sat back with the letter in front of me on the desk and felt grateful.

CHAPTER TWELVE:

Although Dave and I had been friends for years, it was never our custom to visit each other's road crew tents or later our Espero trailers. We'd see each other at work and then meet somewhere public. We were like solitary bucks with solitary bedding areas. We did our own time. But now the sisters were bringing us closer. And so, on payday I decided to walk over to Dave's trailer with a case of beer around 9:00 p.m. and surprise him if he was home. I figured he'd be thirsty and would like to show me some of his drawings and I could fish for info about his phone and Sally. His bedroom light was on, but the rest of the trailer was dark with the living room curtains drawn open and the porch light off. I knew it was his bedroom light because all of the single occupancy trailers had the same floorplan. I stepped quietly up to his door and heard the bed squeaking and thumping and I had my answer. He couldn't wait, and Sally's texts were being deleted. He was crumbling in her mind, and from that minute onwards he started to crumble in my mind too. Just then a driver with his high beams on turned the corner and flashed into Dave's living room and I too was suddenly lit up on Dave's doorstep. He clicked them off when he saw me caught in them and drove to the end of the block and turned again and vanished. Then the squeaking and pounding intensified and a woman started moaning and I silently left and walked back to my trailer.

After a shower, I reread Johnny's first letter. I thought about what Sally had always meant to me and her condition now. And I also thought about being honest with Johnny; and I thought about Dave's pattern with women, his heroin and now sex addictions, and their meaninglessness; and I also thought about his experiences with Sally in the hospital and the hope in his eyes (it was a hope I'd never seen in all the years I'd worked with him); and then I thought about how we found Sally because of him—this was no minor detail—and then I thought who was I to judge him because to be honest that squeaking and pounding and moaning sounded good compared to the silence in my bed, but then I thought, Better that woman than Sally in Dave's bed—Dave probably meant nothing to that woman, she probably wouldn't even remember his name. And then the flash illuminating Dave's living room flared again and was crisply fixed in my mind like an 8" x 10" color print held at arm's length. And as I studied the picture there were no cork boards and pinned drawings or signs of art anywhere, and in a surge it hit me that Dave's opening up *Hell Man* junkie artist disclosure was probably bullshit, and I wondered why he'd bullshit me like that? What could he possibly hope to gain? And then I tried to give him the benefit of the doubt and thought, Maybe he took the sketches down? Or maybe he had them in the bedroom? He did mention drawing the women he laid, and then the bottom line was that he had started banging chicks again and he was not the man for Sally, and so I texted Johnny that night and told her none of the details but simply that Dave had forgotten about Sally, and she should let Sally forget him. "It would be best if he faded away," I wrote. And Johnny texted back, "Okay."

Dave had never referred to Sally as a piece of tail, ever, and because of that we didn't become strangers. The artist in jail story bothered me, though, and I needed closure on that. If it was true, fine, but if he had lied, why? He took me into his confidence, he had me, so much so that I had almost opened up to him about my own criminal record, and now that his story was uncertain I was glad I had kept my mouth shut. I resolved never to mention Sally again. Instead, I'd wait to see whether or not Dave really was a friend.

The following week Dave was rushed into my first-aid station. He had fallen from the second floor of a house he was framing on the east side of the lake. His forehead was bloody and he was unconscious for a while during transport. He wasn't whining about pain. Dave said he had been unusually tired recently and had dozed off during coffee break and fell off the edge of the open wall he was framing. "I see," I said as I cleaned the sand and sawdust out of his wound. His forehead was swelling over his right orbit, and I held a thick cotton pad over his eye as I cleaned the wound with a gauze pad soaked in Bactine. Then I dried the wound and applied a fresh sterile pad and started to gauze and tape it in place. Dave was silent as I worked, but occasionally he looked up at my face as I bandaged him.

Then I said, "Dave, you don't need to bullshit me. I thought we were friends."

"What the fuck are you talking about," he replied in a slow dry voice.

"Your pupils are like pins, man. It's obvious you're using junk again. Why? It fucked you up years ago, why would you go back to it now?"

"Fuck," was his dry whispered reply. "Are we alone?"

"Yeah, and the door is closed," I said. And then he tried to explain.

"I shouldn't have met Sally. She gave me hope. After she took off, I lasted less than a week. I thought about her kisses and everything about her, but it wasn't enough. I just lay in bed with a hard-on every night."

"A compass points north," I said, trying to lighten his confession.

But he responded, "It was pointing at any woman I could find, not Sally. I said to myself, 'Dave, you're a piece of shit, fuck it,' and I went out and got laid. Since she's been gone, I've given up. She's a different species, out of my league."

"She's just been raised Catholic, man. Give it time," I said. "She's probably fighting her own demons. At least try, and if it doesn't work out, it was still good to know her for a while."

"Not good for me, Tom. My cock's in a bear trap. Last week I got hammered and tore down all of my drawings and burned them. I tried to think of Sally, but my brain switched off the light, and I called some old friends in Vancouver. I give the fuck up. I don't care if I die. I'm shit."

"Just because you can't stop banging an endless stream of willing hot chicks doesn't make you shit. You've got to lighten up. This landslide doesn't have to happen."

Dave was breathing deeply and not listening. It was like he was in a tunnel, deaf.

But I continued, "Listen. You've just started using again, I get it, but I'll help you get clean. If you quit, I can slip you some heavy codeine for pain and after a few hard nights, they'll be bitches for sure, you'll be feeling stronger. And then be honest with Sally about the lust thing. She might surprise you and understand. And if she doesn't, move on, maybe care about the women you screw, maybe remember their names and draw them, idealize them in your works, put them in the galleries of immortality," I said hardily and laughed.

"You're full of shit," Dave said with a forced smile.

"Go for it, man. Clean up and then talk to Sally. There's always hope."

I finished up the bandage and Dave gave me a handshake with a slight tremor in it. He forced another smile, and said, "I'll give it all I've got." And then he walked out holding his bloodstained Padres baseball cap which wouldn't fit again until his swelling was down and his bandage was off.

I felt like shit. Dave hadn't lied to me, and he hadn't disrespected Sally. He had just measured himself against her and realized he was nothing, at least that's the way he saw it. He was staggering down a lethal path, and I wasn't sure what to do. My text to Johnny had said, "Let him fade away," and now he was fading away.

I've always defined a friend as someone I can be completely honest with, and I've always said that I can count my true friends on one hand. And Dave seemed to be one of those friends now, and I decided to help him if possible, get him cleaned up and pumped with hope, and then let Sally take it from there.

I immediately phoned Johnny and said, "I misjudged Dave. He's been thinking about Sally constantly and struggling deeply. We should let Sally decide about him in the future."

"I'll keep him in my prayers, Tom."

"And I'll do all I can for him, too."

I didn't hear from Dave over the next few days. He didn't come by for codeine tabs. But when I called the foreman on the east side, he told me he was showing up for work and seemed okay, so I gave him some breathing room. I gave him two more days, and then decided to phone him before walking over with a case of beer. It was 9:00 p.m. and I had the telephone in my hand when I heard a burst of sirens approaching our trailers. They were coming in fast, and when I looked out I could see the spinning red and blue lights of cops and emergency vehicles slicing circles in the night air on Dave's block.

Between the trailer silhouettes, the lights flickered and cut in hot chaotic chops, while the pinkish metal blue of the fading sunset against the mountain edges surrounding Vermilion Lake in the distance looked serene and cool. The lake was a placid gun-metal gray, and above us the sky was thickly peppered with various sizes of stars, a continuum from thick burning dots to barely visible silver glowing powder.

The paramedics were too late. They found Dave dark purple and dead, fallen from his drawing table, with The Velvet Underground blasting their song "Heroin," set on replay. The drawing on the table was large. It showed a man's torso in rough outline and a finished tattoo chest design placed over his heart. It was strikingly detailed and symmetrical, composed of perfectly executed blue roses with a scroll-like ribbon with no words written in it yet. Dave had lightly noted in pencil next to the ribbon, "Use a medieval manuscript font."

When I helped clean out Dave's trailer after the funeral, I took the drawing and kept it. That night I phoned Johnny and told her the full truth about what Dave had been going through and that he was dead. And through tears she said, "I'll have a Mass said for Dave. Sally hasn't mentioned him in weeks and it would be best to let him pass away. Sorrow couldn't possibly help her recovery now. Dave's in God's hands now."

We agreed that we'd scrap the romantic collection of letters idea because we needed to hear each other's voices and really communicate.

"We don't have time for subtle role playing," I said.

"I agree, Tom. We're surrounded by an urgent realism."

Then Johnny added, "But we're also surrounded by an urgent joy. We must live to the fullest."

The whole thing with Sally and Dave and then his death had shaken us. We'd continue to be playful, but we'd be bearing down from now on. We both meant business. And from that point onwards I dreamt of Johnny every night, and she said she dreamt of me. I didn't know it at the time, but I was about to be introduced to a theology of the body that would blow my 100% cotton loose-fit boxers off. And I knew that if I could balance love, first aid, and accuracy, I'd have a shot at being a happy man.

CHAPTER THIRTEEN:

The equipment and crews were starting to work on the ranges at the north rim of the lake, and I was excited but also impatient at having to wait for months to start shooting. Then I got the idea that I might be able to set up a primitive but properly measured practice range in the empty expanses behind Vermilion Lake, the back side of the mountains surrounding the lake. I could borrow a company 4 x 4 and surveying equipment on a weekend and bring some 4 x 8 sheets of ¾ inch plywood to use as target boards and set them up with boulders as support at 1000 meters, and I could use my Black & Decker Workmate as a shooting bench. Once I had some accurate long-range loads worked up and my rifle zeroed, I could shift into prone position as required in official competitions and start to practice sincerely. If I could get out every weekend until the ranges were finished, I figured I'd be in great shape to compete once they officially opened. Will New said he was okay with the idea and was happy to lend me the truck and surveying equipment. I would, however, have to get the local RCMP firearms officer to approve my plan. Basically, I had to submit photos of the area and prove that my line of fire would be absolutely safe. Then I could receive a permit.

I made an appointment, and I saw him the next Saturday at 1:00 p.m. The officer's name was Hank Processi. He was a huge man in his early forties with a thick salt and pepper brush cut, hazel eyes, goatee, massive hands, and genuine smile. He owned an ultra-friendly amber-eyed black lab named Hunter, who never left his side except to greet everyone who came near Hank by licking them until they felt like loved postage stamps. And once they were well licked, he'd melt to the floor in a gesture of absolute trust and stretch out his full length and implore the visitor to scratch his belly. If you rejected his invitation, or accepted it but then stopped scratching prematurely, Hunter would quickly get to his feet and start licking you again. Hunter's owner loved shooting and was an enthusiastic supporter of all lawful firearm use, anything that went bang. Illegal guns were another matter. Hank would come down on any lawbreaker "like a ton of bullet casting lead," he said. And even seemingly minor infractions, committed willfully by a legal gun owner, like taking a legally owned pistol secretly on a hunting trip to shoot grouse or something (hunting with handguns being universally illegal in Canada), were absolutely intolerable for Hank. He'd "smash down his illegal ass," he said, and make sure his gun license was revoked for life. Follow the law, and Hank was happy if you "blazed through a thousand rounds a day," but break it, and he had you in his sights.

I was glad he liked me. And after seeing my documentation and photos he thought my temporary range was a great idea. He even asked if he might come out and shoot with me in the future, and I said of course. He said he had a custom heavy barrel 7mm Remington Magnum rifle that he'd not shot at 1000 meters since his Emergency Response training years earlier in his career. 300 meters, he said, was close range for that gun. "The bullet would hardly even be stabilized at 300 meters," Hank said. He signed the required permit form, and then initialed and stamped with the RCMP seal a map of the area he'd marked a rectangle on with permanent pen. As I thanked him and was leaving he said, "Tom, I almost forgot. Be careful back in that area because a few weeks ago a photographer saw a large grizzly high up back of the mountains there. He took a few long-range photos of the bear, but when it started to stare at him he got the hell out of there quickly, and fortunately the bear didn't follow. He had pepper spray but was unarmed and on foot hiking."

I thanked Hank for the heads up and told him it wouldn't be a problem, "I'll be well armed with a high power rifle, plus have a company 4x4 when I'm back there."

He nodded and said, "Good."

The following weekend I drove to Accurate Rifle Supplies in Prince George to pick up the Sako TRG 42 .338 Lapua Mag rifle (topped with a state of the art

Mark 4 ER/T 8.5-25x50mm Leupold scope), that I ordered as soon as Johnny confirmed that the ranges were officially in the works. The rifle was beautiful, completely finished and stocked in a sand gray flat nonreflective finish. I spent almost all of my savings, close to $10,000, for the complete set up—rifle, scope, shooting glasses, reloading dies, manual press, powder measure, and scale—plus I bought five different powders to experiment with, but only one type of bullet, the Sierra 250 grain Hollow Point Boat Tail MatchKing. I bought a box of 500 for starters, and I was ready to reload.

I cleared all of the junk out of my bedroom in the trailer and built a small but sturdy reloading bench out of two three-foot strips of 1" sanded good one side plywood. I bolted the sheets together onto heavy metal brackets that I then bolted to the exterior wall of the trailer. Then I drilled and bolted down the powder measure and manual press. I installed two foot-wide shelves above the bench and pinned up a Sierra bullet chart poster for atmosphere, and I was ready to go. My Sierra loading manual listed nine loads for the .338 250 grain bullet, but I only worked up the five potentially fastest loads, twenty rounds of each. I started with two grains of powder below maximum for all five powders, and I seated the bullets 5/100ths of an inch deeper than the maximum C.O.L. (cartridge overall length) 3.681, listed in the manuals. Before I started, I set up my camera on a tripod to record the entire process from start to finish, with the intention of forwarding the videos to Johnny who had expressed what seemed to be a genuine curiosity.

She had not been interested in guns and had not learned about them from her dad as Sally had when they were in their early teens, and she didn't realize that reloading was a fine technical art that was critical to successful accuracy, as each action and barrel, regardless of factory consistency, seemed to have a unique vibration point where pressure and speed combined to produce the best pinpoint accuracy and power. A reloader's mission, like that of a husband's, is to find that sweet vibration point and then produce the best ammunition possible for that unique gun.

As soon as I had my first batch of test loads ready, and the videos ready to send to Johnny, I talked to her on Skype and forwarded the videos. I told her that on the weekend I'd be setting up my practice range just in back of the mountains that were in front of us as we sat on our bench while she was visiting the lake. I'd be shooting safely on the other side, and I assured her no projectiles could possibly end up in the development. My range plans had been approved by Hank Processi.

"The lovers will be safe, don't worry," I promised her.

We had a good, intimate discussion, exchanged sincere emotions, and then closed our time. The next day, Johnny phoned me and said she had watched all of the videos, and that although she was not "a gun gal" as such, she was surprised to see the meticulous ritual elements involved in the reloading process: the cleaning of the brass, the rolling in lubricant, the resizing, the drying of the cases with diaper flannel, the seating of the primers, the serious absolute concentration while measuring the powder and seating the bullets. She told me, "The whole process is liturgical. It's almost like you are celebrating Mass." And she said, "Your passion for reloading is a good sign for our relationship. I can see God working in your instinct for ritual." And she again reminded me that she was not now, nor would she ever be some kind of pressure Christian pushing me to convert, because as long as I supported our kids' Catholic education, all would be good in God's love.

And that seemed to be my cue to open up, and so I confessed to Johnny that I missed her physical presence and that my dreams were filled with her. I explained—with photographic clarity—how I had been repeatedly having candlelit, explicit, completely naked dreams of us together.

I told Johnny, "In my recurring dream we are on the verge of consummating our marriage. It is our wedding night and you are on top of me. Your hair is loose and down and your face is perfect through the glowing red wisps and strands."

"Okay," Johnny interjected, and I said, "Should I continue?" To which she responded, "If we are married it would only be natural for you to continue, Tom." Her tone of voice was grounded and sensual.

"You have mounted me and your perfect breasts are like ripe fruits aching to be tasted, and arcing upwards I slowly lick your hard nipples and alternately suck each nipple gently as you moan soft approvals."

"Okay."

"Still continue?"

"Yes."

"And as I catch my breath, I glance towards your open legs mounting me and your perfect curved waist and wide hips and lovely fresh ... and you are a fragrant vine of ecstasy, and you are open to new life and it is your fertile time of the month and as our shared sweet tension rises and our synchronized climaxes approach and are within seconds away there's a blast-like flash and I withdraw and wake up soaked in sweat."

There was a thoughtful silence, and I could hear Johnny breathing.

"Coitus interruptus. Tom, I am so sorry you've been tortured in this way. It may seem funny to you but according to my Catholic faith what you are doing in your dream is not moral."

"Not moral?"

"That's right. If we marry you will be required to finish what you start, both of us will. I've dreamt of you too. Want to hear?"

Obviously I was stoked, and said, "Yes."

"I'm not really sure why, but my dreams have been more symbolic, ethereal, and delicate. Everything has been sublimated into soft and dissolving poetic images, settings, gestures, and even words of poetry sometimes. There have been lots of mists and veils, but no sight of you, Tom. You are not naked, and even your handsome face is never visible."

She continued, "I remember one dream where an evening mist covered a lake as the sun was setting and then a huge tree suddenly broke free from its lakeshore roots and plunged into the lake. There was a tremendous wave and then lesser ripples and then a great calm as the water surface became placid with the tree solid and resting in it with the surface reflecting orange as if the tree penetrating the lake and the water were on fire together and fixed in hot time. In my dreams you get to finish, Tom. I'm so sorry you feel tortured in your dreams. I'm not trying to put you through that."

We decided that night that we needed to physically spend time together. Zero contact simply wouldn't be healthy for seven months or more. I was always at the lake, so Johnny determined that based on her current work obligations she'd be able to visit the lake for one weekend at the end of every month until she came to stay for Christmas. This plan would allow me to shoot on Saturdays and Sundays for three weekends each month, and then enjoy her company for the final weekend of each month. We were excited and agreed on some clear intimacy boundaries in advance so that the time we had together would help our relationship develop, not deteriorate.

We had fun discussing the concept of boundaries, and Johnny drafted the specifics. My body didn't need a map—she'd know what to touch and what not to touch—but her body was a different matter. Because her body was curvaceous and a man's hands tend to naturally follow gravity, these were the boundaries we agreed to for the sake of our future together: I was allowed to touch her neck (including the collar bone area), the full length of her arms, the central portion of her rib cage on either side (an approximately 6" wide strip centered between her breasts and navel), her upper back (not lower), and her knees and below, along her shins to her feet. These zones were open to touch, but not taste—no oral contact. We would kiss each other's lips, but that's all. No gentle sniffing and then kissing behind her ears or along her throat region. Johnny was wise enough to know that if my tongue started anywhere on her skin a fire would ignite that would lead it to places of no return. We agreed that the rest of her body was "off limits" until we were married. Those were her words, which I thought were cute and extremely sexy and chaste at the same time, and I responded by saying, "We'll hang a sign around your neck that reads: OFF LIMITS, BLASTING IN PROGRESS, DO NOT ENTER, FORBIDDEN AREA."

Later, after we had hung up our phones, it uneasily occurred to me that those were the words on the signs we posted ahead of us as we blasted our road into Vermilion Lake, and it occurred to me that Sally should have seen those signs. Certainly they were posted everywhere in the area where the accident occurred. It was strange that she drove right up into the blast area.

CHAPTER FOURTEEN:

With Johnny arriving in three weeks at the end of July, I had time to shoot and was feeling really good about testing the loads in my new rifle. The future was looking fantastic. Early on Saturday morning, I fueled up the green Dodge Ram 4 x 4 that Will said I could borrow, loaded up the plywood I bought, my Workmate bench, the surveying equipment, a cooler full of ice, Perrier water and Cran-Apple juice, ham and Swiss sandwiches and bananas, and drove to the Esso and filled up with regular. Will had said, "Take it, but put gas in it," and I was happy with that.

As I turned onto the first rough exit just outside of town, the sun was rising and the sky was cloudless. It would be a hot day, clear and without wind. A shooter couldn't ask for more. The rough road was rocky, but not extreme, and I bounced over it at a slow speed to not damage the truck. It had been almost a year since I had been back in behind the mountains surrounding the lake, and the long gravel slide areas were much fuller with plants than I remembered. A few colossal boulders the size of logging trucks had broken loose and come down. Those were new, but the rest looked familiar. And you could see for miles back there, jagged edges rising out of softer undulating hills dissolving into the distance, and a green artery of foliage bordering Windhover Creek as it flowed through the gorge cutting through the range and into Vermilion Lake out of sight on the other side. Thinking of Hank's caution, I thought to myself, If there are any grizzlies back here, they'll be close to the creek where there is cover and food and water, not here in the dry open where I am. And I didn't see any grizzly sign that day.

The surveyor laser rangefinder worked perfectly, and I quickly set up my one thousand meter backboards, posted five 18" bullseye targets, then drove back and set up my Workmate shooting bench, bore sighted my rifle, and then cleaned it and pushed a patch soaked in WD-40 through it and was ready to begin. I planned to fire three rounds of each load at each target, determine which two loads looked most accurate, then clean the rifle thoroughly and let it cool; then set up two fresh targets and fire ten rounds at each with the two best loads and see which grouped the tightest; after that test, I'd clean the rifle again and shoot the final seven rounds of each of those best loads at fresh targets and decide which one would be my competition load. Then I would clean the rifle again and go home, and in my spare time load a batch of that best load for future practicing. That was my plan for the day.

The load that eventually produced the best accuracy was a combination of H 1000 powder and a Prov 271 magnum primer with the Sierra 250 grain MatchKing bullet. The final group of seven was the size of a grapefruit (which is incredibly good for 1000 meters) and I was pumped. The day had been an amazing success, and I was excited about the gun and the load. But I was also troubled. Those last seven shots of the day, those best shots, were each accompanied by a flash of Sally's lips, not Johnny's. Just as every dynamite blast on the road into Vermilion Lake vividly evoked the wet taste and presence of Sally's perfect mouth, so did every shot fired. I slowly packed up and drove back to town thinking about this all the way. I was dead to Sally. She looked straight through me, there was nothing to see, I had dealt with that, and Johnny was now the unbelievably perfect woman I was rapidly falling in love with, not a substitute or replacement, but a fresh future hitting me from out of nowhere. My dead fantasies rising from the dead now puzzled me, and I felt guilty. I didn't want to mention anything to Johnny because I figured that explosions had been linked to Sally for so long that I shouldn't expect that conditioned response to vanish overnight. I was like one of Pavlov's dogs. But with time, the association would fade, I thought, and so I determined that to help expedite that erasure when I came out to shoot the next day with a fresh batch of that best load, with each shot that I squeezed off, I would consciously think of Johnny's unbelievable lips, not Sally's. I'd condition myself for my new future.

That night I loaded 40 fresh rounds, then showered and crashed. I got up early on Sunday and was set up at the range by 10:00 a.m. I posted two targets and planned to shoot 20 rounds at one, clean the rifle, and then shoot 20 rounds at the other. Before shooting, I sat there at my bench and looked out at the clear horizon and cloudless sky, and I thought back to the shooting instruction I had received as a younger man, prior to beginning my road crew work 7 ½ years earlier with Horses & Sons.

My old mentor, Jake Wardelle, a wiry, tanned, kind-eyed man, had been a sniper in WW II. I met him at our local gun club, and he took me under his wing. He taught me how to shoot and how to reload. Knowing how to breathe and aim and pull the trigger is a technical art. And as I was mentally preparing to shoot that morning, I recalled his advice:

"When a cartridge is in the chamber and you are breathing slowly in and out and letting the crosshairs in your scope saw consistently through the center of your point of aim, you don't want to hold your breath and tremble, nor do you want to just keeping breathing as you pull the trigger. Instead, breathe naturally as you saw through the target, establish a calm rhythm, and then pause your breath and squeeze when you are exactly at the point of aim you desire. The squeeze is important, and the shot going off should almost surprise you, the pull of the trigger must be gentle."

Then Jake smiled and sincerely advised me, "Don't jerk your trigger. Instead, treat your trigger like you would a nun's breast. Stroke it gently and with reverence."

I'll never forget his irreverent advice. And yet, Jake intended no sacrilege. He was a sensitive man in many ways. Later that day at the gun club, he privately shared a memory that had been burned into his mind as a young sniper in the war:

"Around 15:00 hours, I killed an enemy soldier from a great distance. It was certain. And after the enemy unit had retreated, our troop moved in to investigate the bunker they had been holed up in. I had never checked any of my targets, so I decided to visit my shot. When I entered the bunker I found a sniper maybe 16 years old at the most. The boy had a good head of blonde hair and was lying there dead with a small hole between his eyes."

Jake didn't say if the dead boy's eyes were open or closed, but his enduring trauma at the event seemed to suggest the former.

He went on, "The full-metal jacket ammo required in the military doesn't mushroom like hunting ammo does. It makes a clean small hole, like a drill."

Jake was shocked by his target, but snipers had to be objective and do their job. That boy had an accurate rifle aimed in Jake's direction when Jake shot him. One more breath and a second of hesitation longer and it could have been Jake on the ground, dead at 19 with a clean drill hole in his forehead.

"I continued to kill at long range. It was my duty to obey orders. But I never visited a target again."

As I listened to Jake that day, talking about fondling nuns and suddenly being shot dead, it hit home how strange a tangle life is.

And as I readied myself to shoot that morning, I rehearsed his technical advice. Then I began shooting as he trained me to shoot.

With each of those first 20 rounds, I slowly squeezed the trigger while breathing rhythmically and thinking of Johnny's perfect mouth and how our first kiss at the *Subway* was like Mount St. Helens erupting, and how all of our later kisses were mature, richer, and more delicate. Before each detonation, I closed my eyes and visualized her exquisite symmetrical lips, was calmed by their beauty, and then let them fade to black as I opened both eyes slowly and aligned my Duplex Crosshairs with my target in the distance. The precision and calm of Johnny's mouth shifted to my reticle. And yet, as I thought of her mouth prior to each shot, it ruined my aim. My group of twenty was scattered all over the target like a blast of heavy OO buckshot. I reasoned it was just technical confusion; my old conditioning was kicking in; what I needed was a Zen-like 'no thoughts' approach.

"The last thing any shooter needs to think about is the welcoming mouth of a woman when he's trying to concentrate," I repeated aloud as I thoroughly cleaned my rifle and let it completely cool.

Then I set up to shoot my next 20 rounds trying to think of 'nothing,' and the first three shots weren't even on the board. So as an experiment I fired the next 17 rounds thinking of Sally's mouth. My group was lethal, the size of an apple at 1000 meters, basically impossible.

"Damn," I said aloud.

I had some lunch there at my bench and felt depressed for a while, and then it hit me that if my mind wanted to work that way, and if that made me super-accurate, and if it was only my imagination, and if Sally was essentially gone and all of my real feelings were now for Johnny in reality, then thinking about Sally with each shot was utterly harmless, it didn't mean anything really, and so for the sake of my future with Johnny I should just flow with my conditioning and continue to improve. But this inner concentration technique should be kept secret, no, private was a better word, because Johnny might be hurt by this, like when you are young and you're told to always tell the truth unless doing so might hurt someone's feelings. That was my reasoning.

That night I called Johnny and shared my enthusiasm about my unbelievable apple-size group, and she was pumped to see that I was improving so rapidly. We discussed how between my natural shooting gift and her work as an environmental architect we had promise. In fact, we contemplated a future where we might work together to, as she put it, "globalize new range designs and make 1000 meter shooting as popular as soccer and football and baseball."

"It might have sounded grandiose twenty years ago," Johnny said, "but recent reports and surveys indicate it might work. Young people, especially, are shifting their attitudes about the shooting sports, no longer seeing them as linked to hunting or to war, but instead as linked to Zen and other eastern meditation traditions."

"Absolutely," I said, "1000 meter shooting will also be attractive to youth because our cutting edge globally ubiquitous environmentally friendly ranges will have automatic sand sifting systems built into every berm design so as to ensure zero lead contamination and 100% recycling."

"Yeah," Johnny agreed, "And GREEN T-shirts bearing the slogan—1000 meter shooting is far out—could be mass-produced (and if possible printed in sixteen modern languages) and the movement could take hold of the next generation of shooters. We could end up building an economic empire from scratch with our new range designs."

We had a great talk and were excited about our Plan A, but we also discussed a Plan B.

I said, "Or, we could delete all global business ambitions and keep very close to nature's rhythms at Vermilion Lake."

And she said, "Yeah. I could work as an architect at the lake. That would be plenty."

And I said, "Yeah, and I could shoot twelve times a year and be at home most of the time. We would have all the money we needed for our growing family."

After about an hour of energized discussion our plane seemed to land, and we laughed at how all of our speculations had been ignited by an apple-size group at 1000 meters.

Johnny also mentioned that the state of New York experienced a minor earthquake that day. She didn't feel it, nor did anyone in her immediate vicinity or any of her local friends feel it. But "it was odd that it happened at all." That was "more of a California thing," she said. We affirmed our love sincerely, and both of us were very excited about seeing each other for two days at the end of July.

To be honest, I felt a bit guilty about not mentioning the Sally / shot correlation to Johnny, but what could I say, really? If I was going to be thoroughly honest, would I also tell her that thinking of her mouth threw off my accuracy? It would be ridiculous. I had to be rational and just keep an odd but harmless secret. We were growing stronger as a couple and we were super-attracted to each other. I was open to Catholicism and not pressured at all. Johnny was bit by bit sharing with me the best of Catholic art, music, and theology, plus reinvigorating the whole Motown vibe for me. She was okay with my slow contemplation of her faith, and it looked like us even remaining in different spaces forever would be okay and not an issue in any future we had together. She was leaving our relationship "in God's hands" because she was seeing how her daily struggles to reacquaint Sally with her Catholic upbringing were helping her understand what I was going through. And all of this good stuff was combined with the fact that she was ridiculously beautiful in both body and soul. I was happy.

CHAPTER FIFTEEN:

The Saturday morning that Johnny's plane touched down, the sky was packed with soft clouds. Her plane seemed to suddenly pierce through the white fluff and then land. And when I saw her walking towards me through the arrivals tunnel, it seemed like a dream. No tight bun or designer clothes, but instead, bright pink painted toes in white sandals, tight white jeans, and a powder blue T-shirt, and her shiny red hair down with just a light blue ribbon hair pin at each temple keeping it out of her bright green eyes. When she saw me her face lit up and her smile was fresh. I felt incredibly unworthy of her and flinched at a brief flash of Sally's mouth and my shooting, and then that dissolved and I was back fully in Johnny's presence.

As soon as I could hold her, I gently embraced her and said, "You are a walking dream. It is so good to see you," and Johnny warmly initiated our first kiss. She made it brief and not wet, just a firm pressing together of our lips with a tiny, hardly discernable biting of my bottom lip as she pulled back and said, "So where is my limousine?" and I responded, "You mean the company 4 x 4?"

"Cool, we're going off road?"

I laughed and said, "I hadn't thought of that, but if you're serious, before we get to the lake I could run you back in behind the mountains and show you where I've been shooting. It's beautiful country back there."

"I'd love to see it, Tom. I never gave much thought to what was outside of and behind my design for the lake, and it would be such a nice change from the streets of New York. I've felt so pressed in since I last saw you."

"Done. And don't worry, I'll protect you from any grizzlies."

"Grizzlies. Are you serious?"

"Absolutely. I've not seen one yet, but others have."

"I trust that you'll keep us safe, Tom."

We got her luggage and within half an hour we were in the truck and on the highway. I felt the time was right, so I said, "Do you think it's too soon for me to be listening to 'My Girl,'" to which she smiled and said, "As long as I can listen to 'Heatwave.'"

"But it's The Temptations. You recall our intimacy control plan, right?"

"Of course," and Johnny clicked open a small case she had kept in the cab of the truck, rather than in the box with the rest of her luggage, and pulled out a scroll-like roll of paper. She partially unrolled it and said, "Here's the map I made for you."

"Are you serious?" I said, and then put on my right turn signal and pulled off the highway and clicked on my emergency flashers, so I could look at her map properly. It was wild. Obviously, Johnny was a first-rate drawer and had access to state of the art graphic design technology at work, because the unfurled paper contained four line drawings portraying her body from the front, the back, and the left and right side views. The pictures were beautifully detailed and anatomically exact to her body shape. Just glancing at the left side-view diagram, my eye instantly noticed the exact curve of her neck and the proportions of her slightly upturned left breast and its firm nipple. It was the exact silhouette that I had remembered photographically after seeing her in that summer dress during our four days together. And on these beautiful drawings were imposed, as on any map, clear boundaries—the clear intimacy boundaries we had agreed upon. The areas I could touch were a soft pink color, and the no entry zones were left blank white. The boundary lines were drawn with sharp thin black ink. There were no blurry watercolor-like edges anywhere.

As we were parked there with the emergency lights blinking, Johnny held the scroll up against the roof of the cab so all four diagrams were visible and smiled widely at me and said, "Am I an organized lover, or what?" And burst out laughing.

I looked at her in partial disbelief, but then I remembered how smart she was and said, "I can't believe you actually created those maps of your body. I'm especially happy to see all of that pink territory just aching for a pioneer like me to explore."

"It's rugged and wild country, Tom, but I'm confident you're man enough to handle it," she said and laughed.

She rolled the scroll back up and slid a thick pink elastic down to its center and clicked it back into her case and then sat back with the wind blowing in her hair, and her left hand tucked in wild strands as I pulled back out onto the highway and accelerated and pushed play on my Temptations CD and "My Girl" started and we had sunshine on that day as we drove on.

As we took the turnoff to Vermilion Lake, all of the emotions we shared there on Johnny's previous visit flashed back at me—the happy discovery of Sally, the shock that she had become a memoryless shell of her former self, the ache when she looked through me like an invisible stranger, and the unexpected sudden freedom to let my heart fall towards Johnny and her sudden freedom to open herself to me without being unkind to the sister she had always loved without limit. And I recalled how we stopped for lunch that day and the kisses and intimacy we shared and how we laid the foundation for our new lives together, and so I asked Johnny if she wanted to eat lunch at the same spot again or at my range, and she said, "At your range would be good."

As we drove along that flat new road to Vermilion Lake, all of the nights and blasts and scenes and countless injuries and dreams and camping along that direction over seven years of work, and the strange culmination at the lake with Johnny's visit, and the car show and that Shelby in what seemed like a rushing steelhead river, flashed through my mind like the reflections shot from steelhead explosively flashing their chrome sides in deep green pools after violently hitting Gibbs-Delta Croc copper fire wing spoons. And I felt good as we drove. The sky above us was brightly lit by the sun. The sunshine radiated through the clouds and they looked like colossal fluffed up mounds of the bulk first-aid cotton that is used behind large sterile pads and wrapped tensors to slow the bleeding of head wounds. And the blue sky looked refreshing and cool against the jagged mountain edges in the distance.

After my Temptations CD finished, she asked if I wanted to hear a song or two from her Gregorian chant CD, and I said sure. She introduced the first piece, which she said was medieval, around the 13th century. The piece was called "Stabat Mater." It described the sorrow in the heart of a mother facing the unbearable death of her only child. And Johnny said the masculine beauty of the piece was stunning in her opinion, and she said her favorite lines in the text were, "Quis est homo qui non fleret, / matrem Christi si videret / in tanto supplicio?" Which she translated from the Latin as, "Who is the man who would not weep to see the mother of Christ in such suffering?" As Johnny explained these details to me, it hit me that she really believed that deep in every person was a soul capable of love, no matter how hardened that person had become. I respected her for that, but I wasn't yet convinced that she was right. We listened to that chant and a few others as we drove, and like before, we moved through a natural cathedral with the rolling dry hills and Windhover Creek's winding green edge in the distance.

The CD had finished and we had been silent for a few minutes when I said, "There's the turnoff to my range," and pointed.

"Cool," Johnny said.

And as I glanced at her, she was smiling and had given up on controlling her hair. Her passenger window was all the way down and her long hair was swirling and wafting and seemed to be longing for a cool bedroom pillow to spread out on and come to rest on and then be smoothed away from her face by my fingers. And we turned onto the road and slowed right down and bumped and rocked towards the edge and then behind the mountains surrounding Vermilion Lake. Johnny was fascinated by the look of the area, its pristine details never having known dynamite or human road builders. I pulled the truck right up to the spot where I usually set up my Workmate shooting bench and pointed to the 4 x 8 sheets of plywood set up in the distance at 1000 meters.

It took a few seconds for her eyes to focus and then she said, "You can shoot that far? No way."

And I responded, "Accurately."

And with my hands I indicated the apple-sized group I had last shot there. She was stunned, obviously, and it seemed that for the first time she realized that I really could make a good living as a professional target shooter and that our previous colorful dreaming was more grounded than she had imagined.

As we sat on the tailgate looking out into the vast expanse of my range and the empty spaces fading out into the distance behind my target boards, we ate the ham and Swiss sandwiches I had made and washed them down with one-liter bottles of ice-cold chocolate milk from my camp cooler.

I smiled at her and she said, "What?"

"I'm the journalist. Here comes my interview. Okay?"

"Sure. Go for it," Johnny responded and smirked.

"This is Thomas Tems reporting from behind Vermilion Lake Village. I'm speaking today with Ms. Johnny Nostal, the creative mind behind this entire development. Ms. Nostal, how did a nice girl like you end up designing an entire development in a beautiful place like this?"

"You really want to know? You might find the answer a bit theoretical and dry."

"I'm sure our viewers are not afraid of dry, Ms. Nostal."

"Okay. I began with the concept of sustainable beauty. That sounds like a makeup commercial, I know, but it's not. In graduate school, I immersed myself in environmental theory, in particular the theories of Komociama and Warrdekay. The plan for Vermilion Lake—the residential lot plans and the balanced larger / smaller cabin zoning plan, the road systems, the waterworks and drainage, plus the green corridors system—is based on mirroring the balance already inherent in nature, that is, a benign explosion of diversity contained by the biosphere's law of harmonized equilibrium. Does that make sense?"

"So far, absolutely. I'm not surprised that your thoughts are beautiful."

"Never mind that," Johnny said as she rocked her shoulders in a one, two, three, four pattern, then smiled and continued playing her live TV role.

"There's more. The aerial photographs of the lake surprised me, and once I examined the topographical maps and saw the unique symmetry of the contour lines surrounding the lake, the full-scale layout for the lots suddenly came to me. I felt the pattern, as if it was latent in the lakeshore, submerged and waiting to be recognized. I sensed the owners would love their land and not want to leave. They'd want to really live there, not just visit. And I didn't imagine we'd have to force the environment. Rather, I sensed it would intimately welcome us in."

"A natural destination for lovers?"

"Yeah."

"Is that enough theory for your viewers?"

"That's perfect, Ms. Nostal. That's a wrap, Joe!"

We both laughed aloud, and Johnny said, "Pass me a peach please, Tom."

I reached one out of the cooler and said, "There you go."

We each ate a cold peach, and Johnny asked with a smirk, "Why are you watching me eat?"

Her lips were alluring beyond words and watching her bite into that peach and seeing the sweet juice dripping down her chin was too much for me, and I said with a wide smile, "Let's just say, if we're going to wait until we're married, I better not pack fresh peaches again."

To which she replied, "Canned peaches in heavy syrup are excellent. Let's eat those while we're dating, and save the fresh peaches for later, okay?"

"It's a deal," I said and smiled, but just then I noticed something on the gravelly ground about fifty yards down range.

"What do you see?" Johnny asked, wiping her face and hands with a clean wet cloth from the cooler and then slipping from the tailgate to walk alongside me.

"I'm not sure yet, hang on. Please wait here at the truck."

When I got there I saw a massive pile of fresh grizzly bear shit, a huge pile filled with seeds, not garbage, and massive prints indicating the bear had walked right through my range on his way to Windhover Creek. The scat wasn't steaming, but it was far too fresh for us to be hanging around unarmed.

I had no gun or pepper spray, and I said to Johnny, "Please get in the truck, we should leave this area right now."

"Why? What is that stuff?"

"It's fresh grizzly shit. I shouldn't have brought you here without a gun."

She riveted me with her green eyes and said, "Whatever you say, Tom," and we both got in the truck, fired it up and headed back to the main road. Once we'd turned back onto the highway, I said, "I'm sorry I put you at risk. I wasn't thinking. If we go back there again, I'll be sure to bring a gun so you'll be safe." I promised her.

I didn't say more, but as we drove I thought to myself, I must never let Johnny's beauty distract me again. That was my problem, not hers. I was to blame for taking my mind off of the realities of existence, the dangers that are real.

Within thirty minutes we were at the lake and Johnny was checked into Gold Motel, but this time her room was on the second floor, top right side, with a nice balcony overlooking the lake in the distance. We agreed that she'd have some time to nap and shower and freshen up and then we'd have dinner at the new candlelight-style Italian restaurant just up the hill on the road where the car show was during her last visit. The new place was called Luigi's House, and though formal clothing was not required, we decided that we'd both dress for the occasion: look as good as possible in the candlelight we reasoned and smiled. I'd pick her up at 6:00 p. m., we'd eat, and then walk along the lake shore and finish at our bench and be close. Then I'd take her back to her motel room where we had agreed we'd allow ourselves exactly thirty minutes of affection with Johnny's map unfurled and pinned to the wall in front of the couch we'd be sitting on. The pink access zones were clearly marked and we were ready to take our relationship to the next level.

CHAPTER SIXTEEN:

When I arrived at her motel at 6:00 p.m., the sky had cleared. For most of the afternoon, a fresh wind had been gently pushing the massive clouds far out of sight onto the horizon and beyond, and now the sky above us was a clean fresh blue. I knocked on her motel door and when she opened it, I was stunned.

She stared back for a minute and then said, "What?"

"What?" I replied with a dry mouth.

She was wearing a white crochet dress that reached just above her knees and had a collar neckline and short sleeves. It was elegant and simple. Her silky red hair was up in a beautiful loose bun and she was wearing small, platinum and emerald earrings that looked like green flowers. The earrings matched her eyes.

"The *what* is the miracle of seeing you. You truly look lovely."

"Thank you, Tom," she said with a playful smirk. "Brace yourself for the female gaze. Let me *beep* your barcode. You look wonderful too standing there muscular and handsome in your polished tan brogues, new black Levis, white dress shirt, and chocolate brown sports coat matching your brown eyes (which my mom would probably caution me about, calling them 'bedroom eyes'), and your thick black hair combed back and just curly enough to run my fingers through, and your handsome face and jawline and handsome mouth. Yes, Mr. Tems, I'd say you look fine as well. Perhaps we should make our entrance at Luigi's now, I'm starving," she said and grinned.

The restaurant was a short drive up the hill on Milagro Street, and as we pulled into the parking lot I saw Hank Processi in a white Dodge Ram RCMP pickup. He was in the cab using the police radio as I parked next to him, and I waved through the glass as I shut off my engine.

"That's Hank," I said to Johnny as we both unbuckled our seatbelts. "The officer who approved my range. Let's quickly say hi before we go in, okay? He's a good guy and his dog is really something."

"Sure," Johnny said as she slid out and closed her door and started to walk around our pickup to Hank's truck. Hank was off the radio now, and he was rolling down his window to greet us. Johnny took my hand, and as we walked alongside Hank's 8 foot box, I saw that he had Hunter with him in a large wire dog crate.

"Hey, Hunter. How you doin' fella!" I said to him.

Hunter made a low friendly bark and Johnny saw him in his crate. She became rigid and held my arm tight.

"Let's leave, Tom. Let's leave."

Hunter barked again, this time standing up in his crate and wagging his tail, as if he expected us to unlock his crate and let him run free.

"Tom, please. Let's leave."

"He's super-friendly, Johnny. There's nothing to be afraid of."

Hank looked at his dog through his open cab window and yelled, "Hunter, quiet boy!"

Then he looked at Johnny and said with a smile, "Don't worry, he's just saying hello. That's how he talks."

Then Hank chuckled as Hunter lay down in his crate and stopped barking.

"Beautiful dog, eh? And smart too," I said.

But Johnny was trembling now and holding my arm so tight that it almost hurt.

She pulled me close and firmly whispered into my ear so Hank couldn't hear her, "Please. Please take me away from here."

I was startled by her expression.

"Sorry. We've got to run, Hank. Good to see you boy," I said to Hunter.

And then we immediately walked away from Hank's truck. I gave a slow single wave as if nothing had really happened. With a blank expression, Hank gave me a quick nod with his RCMP ball cap as if to say, Best to forget whatever that just was. Then he fired up his truck and pulled out of the parking lot holding his radio microphone in his right hand while steering with his left. Hunter was invisible, submerged in his dog crate in Hank's box, but as Hank turned out of the parking lot, Hunter suddenly stood up in his crate and his amber eyes looked at us and he woofed a final friendly acknowledgement. But Johnny was looking away.

With Johnny's arm still tightly gripping mine, we silently walked around the corner and up onto Milagro Street. As we passed the doorway of a closed shop next to the entrance to Luigi's, I said to Johnny, "Come in here for a second. Let me hold you."

I embraced her. She was still trembling.

"It's okay. You're safe now. The dog is not going to hurt you."

Johnny's breathing decelerated and I could feel her relaxing and softening in my arms.

"I'm so sorry, Johnny. I didn't know you were afraid of dogs. Hunter would never hurt you," I said. And then to cheer her up, "Worst case scenario he'd lick you to death."

Johnny let out a slow, sincere sigh.

"I'm not afraid of dogs, Tom. I love dogs. We had a black lab when we were kids. Her name was Frisky. I don't know what happened back there."

People were walking past us in both directions, so we moved deeper into our store entrance shelter.

"Are you all right? Do you still want to get some dinner?"

"I'm fine, Tom. Really."

She paused and her eyes seemed to freshen.

"Like I said, I'm starving," and she tried to smile.

Then Johnny gave me a long hug.

"I just need your strength, Tom."

As she held me and pulled me in close, I could feel her heart beating, and with her cool hair against my face I held her and her scent and softness were beautiful. We just rested there together for a few minutes and then relaxed our embrace and left our shelter and walked next door and entered Luigi's.

I'd called earlier to make reservations and the headwaiter escorted us to our table. The place was nice: authentic Italian décor throughout, beeswax candles burning in straw basket Chianti bottles on each table, and an accordionist slowly meandering through the restaurant playing very softly, open to requests, but otherwise serenely working through a rich set of memorized classics. Occasionally smiling and in a classy, gentlemanly tone he introduced himself to us as Lorenzo, and he wished us "young lovers" God's blessings. He referred to Johnny as *signorina* and then continued his soft playing and even slower meandering, professionally balancing his presence and availability while honoring the romantic privacy of all of Luigi's guests.

Now that we were seated, Johnny completely relaxed back into her healthy self and said, "I'm fine now, Tom. Thank you for your patience with me. It is so beautiful here. Let's enjoy ourselves."

"If only this balance of the senses could be held forever, eh? Sight, sound, smell, taste," I said in a quiet voice to Johnny across from me in the candlelight, so glad that she was at peace again.

"Maybe it can be held, Tom," Johnny responded, and she slowly reached her hand across the table to mine, her soft green eyes warmly searching my eyes.

We had a delicious meal and drank Chianti and talked in the candlelight and then left for a walk by the lake.

Johnny had brought a small white bag into the truck with her when we left, and at the lake she changed out of her white heels into white sneakers and wrapped a thin white cashmere shawl over her shoulders. She looked ready to walk. It was around 7:30 p.m. and the sky was still bright. The sun was to our right at a 45 degree angle and nearing the mountain edges. A light, cool breeze was caressing the lake and its surface looked like a dull mirror struggling to reflect the sky. We walked slowly along the lakeside path, my hands in my pockets and her left arm through my right arm.

"It's like a dream having you back at the lake. Thank you so much for flying out."

"It's like a dream for me too, Tom. I've been thinking about you constantly, and to touch you now and see you again is strengthening me. I don't feel as rooted when you are far away. It's funny, because I've always thought of myself as a complete and self-sufficient woman, and I am in many ways, but ever since I first met you I've felt more connected. You are the wilderness to me, Tom."

"The wilderness?"

"Yeah. When I was a girl, I'd sometimes feel it when I was steelhead fishing with Mom. The sun and water and everything around us green and fresh and rushing and the fish following their instincts and working upstream to their destinies—eagles circling above them as they finned below in the deep green pools—destinies wired into their DNA, destinies they couldn't alter—the wilderness inside them."

"I'm like that to you?"

"Yeah. I feel really natural with you. I sense we have a destiny to be together until death, to enjoy and support each other and have children together. I hope that doesn't scare you off."

"Not at all, no pressure," I said and grinned.

She held my arm firmly. When we reached our bench we sat down and snuggled close to each other. It was cooling off and Johnny adjusted her shawl, and I pulled her closer to receive the warmth of my body. Our feet were stretched out in front of us and we relaxed back and looked upwards into space. Stars of various sizes burned in the dome above us.

Eventually, Johnny said softly, "Time is a mystery, isn't it, Tom? Here we are, together."

"Yeah. I can't express how good it feels just to be next to you now."

We both looked upwards in silence for another few minutes. Then we saw an elderly couple wearing sweat suits walking briskly towards us. They had their Golden Retriever on a long leash, and it came over to us as they went by. Johnny quickly loved it up by scratching behind its ears while it wagged its tail. And then its owners, anxious to stay on pace, said, "Come on, Smudge," and the retriever rushed back to his owners and walked alongside them and away.

"I love dogs," Johnny said, looking into my eyes and shrugging.

Then she suggested we go up to her motel room for some private time together there. As we ascended the stairs to her room, we were bathed in the faint gold lighting that had just automatically turned on. We could hear the neon humming as it was warming up and brightening. She unlocked her door and we went in together. I noticed the large map on the wall and said, "So there it is?"

"Yeah. We'll try our best, Tom. It will be fun."

When Johnny announced that she was going to slip into something more comfortable, I was not quite sure what to expect. I also felt like I was in a scene that had been played thousands of times in movies, and yet our relationship didn't at all have that cookie-cutter feel to it. Johnny was out of sight in the bedroom, and then in its adjacent bathroom, for about 10 minutes until she said, "Are you ready, Tom?" and I said, "Ready for Human Geography 500."

Then she came out and walked straight to the roast timer on the stove and set it to 30 minutes and clicked it on and it began ticking. No romantic background music, no candlelight, just all lights on and a roast timer ticking. It was not a movie scene. Johnny was wearing a full jogging suit—thick gray jogging pants and a thick gray long-sleeved hoodie zipped right up to the neck. The only skin visible was her face, hands, and bare feet. But her hair was down and loose, and she looked unbelievably good. She could stop traffic in greasy coveralls, I thought to myself.

She plopped down with a bounce next to me on the couch and said, "Something more comfortable," and laughed.

"Okay, let's get to work."

To which she replied, "Yes, to work."

I had removed my sports coat when I first came in, and now Johnny unbuttoned my shirt and reached up across my chest and was caressing my collar bone and lower neck as she moved close and kissed me with her wet mouth and delicately licked and lightly bit the edge of my lip. I tried to caress her arms and rib cage and even her knees as we were kissing, but there was so much thick cotton between my nerves and her skin that all I could feel was her basic structure. So I then subtly reached under her sweat top and slowly put my left hand on her bare rib cage, exactly in the zone she had drawn on the chart, and there I tried to caress her skin so lightly that my touch would be barely discernable.

She said softly, "Your touch is so gentle, Tom."

The roast timer was ticking and there wasn't much more I could explore in that small zone, so I withdrew my hand and slowed my kissing and then pulled back slightly and said to Johnny, "Please don't be offended, but with all that clothing on I just can't feel you. It's like you're inside an arctic sleeping bag or something."

She burst out laughing and said, "Okay. Let me stop the timer and try something a little lighter."

"Sounds good," I said.

And after only a couple of minutes she came out again. This time she had on white pajamas. They were pretty and buttoned only in the middle so that her lower tummy and most of her upper chest were visible, just as she would normally button her pajamas for comfort's sake when sleeping in them.

She asked, "Is this a little better, Tom?" to which I replied, "Oh yeah."

The whole scene looked promising now, and with a smile of approval and a fresh glance at the map on the wall, I suggested we try to get close again. With a playful wiggle she walked over to the timer and clicked it on for our final 15 minutes of controlled intimacy. It was good. The pajamas were super thin soft flannel and she wasn't wearing a bra or panties and she smelled unbelievably good and felt unbelievably soft. It was like a dream. I reached under her PJ top to my allowed rib zones and over her breasts to my allowed collar bone zone and then inside her top down her arms as far as I could until the fabric tightened and blocked me, and then back to her ribs and then out again and gently caressed her knees and down to her feet. Then I left the couch and knelt in front of her and gently moved her knees together and then caressed her shins and held her feet and lightly caressed them. I'd never touched her feet before and she really liked it and rested back and relaxed on the couch and let her knees slightly part and then widen a bit more as she relaxed, and then I kissed her knees gently through the flannel and slowly sat back up on the couch next to her. She smiled a smile of deepening love and appreciation and snuggled closer, and as I held her there with her fresh hair against my chest, I heard the timer ticking and looked up at its big black and white numbers showing we only had three minutes left and then I looked down at Johnny's slightly parted legs and her slightly unbuttoned top and saw her navel and knowing it was in a no entry zone hovered my hand over it as I moved up and back to her full access rib zone, and delicately let my hand caress her there, and the ticking seemed to get louder and I looked down Johnny's PJ top and then at her breasts and through the thin flannel her nipples were clearly like hard wild strawberries, firm and pink, and I couldn't resist and I made a choice. I slid my hand gently from her ribs upwards to hold her breast fully and feel the unbelievable contrast of her soft breast and firm nipple in my hand. I gently caressed her there, knowing full well I was in a no entry zone, and I expected Johnny to flinch and pull back, but she didn't.

She responded to my soft touch with an even softer moan and kissed me very wetly and deeply and inserted her tongue between my lips in slow small thrusts and pulled me strongly towards her. Then she made one last small thrust of her tongue, and a wet sticky withdrawing sound as she stopped kissing my mouth, and then deliberately kissed my cheek firmly and wetly and pulled slightly back and I softly withdrew my hand from her breast and moved it down her tummy and out of her PJ top and held it gently against her face and looking into her green eyes that were starting to water slightly said, "You are so beautiful, Johnny. I'm so sorry. I just couldn't hold myself back. I am aching for you. Dreaming about you."

The roast timer went off and she jumped up and silenced it and came right back. Through the tears that were forming in her eyes she answered, "You're a beautiful man, Tom," and she gently kissed my face, next to my eye, then my cheek, then the edge of my mouth, and then looked at me and smiled softly and ran the tip of her index finger—her nail was painted dark pink with a light pink cross in the center (until that gesture, I hadn't even noticed her nails that evening)—along the edge of my upper lip and said to me in an honest voice, "Every fiber of me wants to act on my desires and give you the green light, Tom. Every fiber wants to tear down that map and burn it in our passions, but my mind insists on asking whether or not right now, tonight, you really want to marry me and father children?"

It was a question passionately asked, and she was a wise woman to ask it, because I was as hard as a granite core sample and not exactly rational at the moment. As Dave had said to me when he was alive, "No man with a hard-on is thinking about the future. Having a woody blinds a man." And that night I was a thick buck steelhead driven against the current to explode upstream at the command of my DNA. The wilderness. Unmarried wilderness.

I answered her, "I trust your judgment, Johnny. All I know is I am falling crazy in love with you. I don't want anything to spoil what we have. I don't want to wake up and find the dream is over."

The word dream seemed to trigger a reaction and she let her tears flow, and I was afraid I'd hurt her deeply somehow. She was trembling and said, "I know I am strange, Tom, and I know other women would never torture you as I am doing, but I am different, I can't help it."

She was weeping and breathing deeply and vulnerable there on the couch.

"I wouldn't blame you if you went with other women. I'm so sorry I can't give you what you need. You deserve to be satisfied."

There was a pause.

"You're a good man, Tom," she said forcing a smile and then genuinely laughing as if at her own medieval eccentricity.

At that instant the lust in me was suddenly detonated: the granite blasted into dust. I felt a surge of strength.

"You're all I want, Johnny. We'll make it."

She stopped crying and held me tight on the couch. Then we stood together at her window facing the lake and the sun was an orange blanket reflecting in the calm surface of the water, and the knife-like edges of the surrounding mountains were softened in the warm glow as night was falling. And then Johnny pulled the drapes closed and we stood there holding each other tight. It was certain in our faces as we smiled and held and supported each other there that night. We had something, and we would be loyal.

Her tears were wiped away now, and as she stood there clearly relieved at our exchange of emotions, she grinned and suddenly stuck out her chest knowing full well that doing so would make stark the silhouette of her breasts and especially highlight her protruding nipples, and said to me in a sassy and playful tone to dispel any dark clouds that might be lingering in my mind, "If providence leads us to marry, Mr. Tems, I can assure you that every day you will be free to explore, to taste, to feel, and to enjoy to the full whatever good gifts the Lord has bestowed on me," winking and with both hands motioning from the top of her head to her toes and doing so while quickly giving her rump a wiggle, "and all within the reasonable guidelines of Canon Law," she said and laughed.

I had no idea what Canon Law was (perhaps a military code or something), so I anticipated the worst and seriously asked, "Even as man and wife we'll have to drive with the parking brake on? Won't that stretch the hell out of the cable?"

To which Johnny laughed and responded, "Just a few taps on the brakes on a few dangerous corners. You'll get all the satisfaction you can handle, Tom. I guarantee it."

It was cute to see her trying to be brazen because as she said this she blushed. This was my cue, and so I recalled an excerpt from her catalogue of marital pleasures: "So, you are guaranteeing me right here and now that once we are married I will have the freedom on a daily basis to taste and explore your perfect body?" And I said the word *taste* slowly with a smile indicating an intense savoring as I glanced at her slowly from head to toe and back again to her eyes sparkling at me.

To which she replied, "Yes, Tom, we'll be happy."

And then she smiled and fluttered her PJ top away from her skin and fanned herself indicating things were getting hot and we should probably say good night for now.

We shared a final kiss and I said, "You are a miracle to me, Johnny. Sweet dreams."

"And sweet dreams to you too, Tom."

As I drove back to my trailer, I detoured past Johnny's bare lot and parked next to it for a moment and left the motor running. Across from it on the horizon was a soft wisp of orange light dissolving. Then I drove home. After I parked, I looked up and the sky was bluish black and the clouds were thickening and a few stars burned through the gaps in the closing clouds. Then I went in and showered and fell asleep.

CHAPTER SEVENTEEN:

A loud banging on my trailer door woke me. I thought it was a neighbor and there was a fire and my detectors had not gone off, but then a woman started shouting and calling out repeatedly, "Dave, are you in there?" I jumped out of bed and pulled on my jeans and went to the door and turned on the porch light to see who the hell it was. I had never seen her before. She was a young woman around twenty-five and obviously very drunk. I looked at my watch and saw it was 2:14 a.m., so I opened the door and said, "Dave's not here. Please stop yelling. You'll wake the whole block." "Where is he?" she slurred and staggered and reached for the porch arm rail to steady herself. I was waking up and it hit me that the bars must have just closed and she was probably one of Dave's distant one-night stands who had found herself lonely and needing a place to crash and so was looking Dave up in the hope that he might be alone.

"Dave doesn't live here," I said.

"Are you Tom?"

"Yeah. How do you know my name?"

"The last time I saw Dave he gave me your address. He said, 'If ever you can't find me, my best friend Tom will know where I am.' Dave's trailer looks abandoned and I thought he might be here with you. Dave wrote me this letter ... " she said, and then started fumbling through her purse dropping her cigarettes and match booklets and Kleenex and bits of junk on the porch.

It looked like she was ready to stumble down the stairs as she tried to coordinate her searching for the letter with the challenge of standing in high heels, and so I said, "Why don't you come in for a minute. We should talk."

"Yeah," she said as she stopped searching and gathered her senses to enter without tripping.

I turned on the living room light which made us both flinch and squint in the brightness and I motioned towards the couch and said, "Please sit down for a minute."

She said, "I'm Carol. Here it is," as she pulled the letter out of her open purse and then plopped down with a bounce on the couch and began to open the letter.

In the bright light, I could see her clearly. She was around 24 or 25, maybe 5'6" tall, long blonde disheveled hair, very attractive face with heavy makeup, especially large eyelashes and bright red lipstick, firm natural breasts under a tiny pink tank top, and super-short blue jean cutoffs, and at the end of her tanned legs she had on navy blue high heels.

"Dave and I broke up a couple of months ago," she said in a slow drawl, the booze almost stronger now that she was out of the fresh air, but then she smiled lopsidedly and said, "But then last month he sent me this letter saying he loved me and needed me. See," she said, holding it up towards me. I could read the words, "Dear Carol. I've been thinking about how we kissed that night ... "

She was drunk. She seemed stunned and impressed that Dave would contact her at all, let alone express affection and love.

"Guys never write love letters nowadays, unless ... [something] ... ," she mumbled.

But Dave seemed sincere in his letter. She explained that they had met in a bar in Prince George a few months back and then "had a great time" together back at her place, which in Dave's terminology would mean that he got lucky and banged her and then forgot her, not caring and assuming she had no actual feelings for him or any other guy she got lucky with. This made Dave's giving out of my address and writing her a love letter all the stranger in my mind. Then it occurred to me that maybe it was a setup. With Dave's twisted sense of humor, he might have been giving out my address and writing love letters to her and other one-nighters just to bring them back to me and get me onto his wisdom. He always told me that I needed to "get with reality," which to him meant realize that old-school love was dead and annihilated for good. "Start fucking with a clear conscience. Follow every rush," he had always advised me.

But who was I to judge Dave? He'd wrestled with his heroin demons long before women became his free dope. And maybe he did change as he was nearing the end. Maybe he imagined himself in a perpetual nod while loving only one woman—Carol, chosen out of the long list—and perhaps the letter was honest.

I sat at the opposite end of the couch shirtless in my jeans in the bright light, and as Carol slurred more details about the letter I politely said firmly, "Carol," to which she paused and looked at me, "I need to tell you that Dave died almost a month ago. He overdosed on heroin. He's buried at the edge of town in the new cemetery. He's the only one there."

I expected an exaggerated drunken spiel, but instead, Carol slowly lifted her hands to her face and cried very softly awhile and then softly repeated a few times the words, "It was too good to be true." It was moving. She explained that she had been a party animal for years and long ago lost count of how many guys she had slept with. At first she hoped for love, but then she soon became hardened and realistic. It was a world of booze and dope and lust, why pretend otherwise?

"Dave's dead, fuck everything. How stupid could I be?" she said as she tore his letter in half. "Got any beer?"

"Yes, but that's the last thing you're getting from me."

"What's the first thing?" she said and lopsidedly smiled at me. "Life goes on, fuck it. You're cute, Tom."

Almost 30 seconds of mourning for Dave, I thought to myself—so much for lingering heartache and the history of romantic art. But then I thought, she is a beautiful woman who has never been truly loved. She hasn't had a chance.

"Carol," I said standing up in the bright room, "I need to call you a cab."

She stood up too and walked over close to me and with a cool hand on each of my biceps said, "A cab to where, Tom? I live in Prince George and the friends I came with have all driven back without me. I need to sleep somewhere tonight. Couldn't I sleep here with you?"

Her blue eyes were sincere, and as she stood there close to me with her hands on my biceps she grinned at me waiting for the inevitable yes which would emerge from my lips any second. She'd never met a man who said no to a promise of certain pleasure. She moved her hands from my biceps to my pecs and then very delicately moved her fingertips down my abs towards my belt. She looked down at my groin and then up to my eyes and with a big smile said, "It looks like the answer is yes?" Her body looked succulent in those tiny shorts and tank top, and granite was definitely forming in my pants. Then I noticed the gold chain that reached to just between her breasts, and I read the italicized words engraved on her heart-shaped medallion: *I swallow*. Fuck, I thought to myself. Then I instantly became embarrassingly hard. I had not touched her or encouraged her in any way. My hands were drooping at my side passively as she stood there inches in front of me offering her scent to me. I could still get out of this, and I had not yet mentioned that I was in love and in a relationship and that Johnny was only a few blocks away sleeping.

Carol saw my reaction to her medallion and smiled, "You look yummy, Tom. It would be fun. I promise not to bite," and she wiggled her breasts and rump.

That was all I could take. I nearly blew my load right there in my jeans. I turned away suddenly and went into my bedroom and came out with a T-shirt on and said in a serious clear voice, which surprised her given our hot context, "Thank you for your willingness to share yourself with me, Carol. Seriously, you are a beautiful woman, and I appreciate your offer. Please don't be offended, but I am in love, and I could never relax and enjoy you knowing that I was being disloyal to my best friend."

Tears welled up in Carol's eyes, and she said, "Disloyal?" as if it were a strange word her ancient soul had not heard spoken in centuries.

Then it hit me that I could drive her to any local motel, that would get rid of her, but then I thought that that would be treating her like some kind of malignant succubus, which she was not. And it hit me that if a decent guy actually loved her and stayed loyal to her, that she might be satisfied in a way that would make the sexual fare she was used to seem like bread and water punishment compared to the finest cuisine at Luigi's House, and she'd be hooked on the good stuff from then on. Also, if I just dumped her off she might get hit on or worse by drunks or whatever. She deserved security and love. She couldn't stay with me, but she could in theory stay with Johnny.

I asked Carol to rest on the couch while I made a call, and from the privacy of my bedroom with the door closed I phoned Johnny at Gold Motel. She was surprised that I woke her and more surprised still by the bizarre night I was having, but she listened and then said, "Of course, bring her up right now. I'm in a huge bed. We can share it, and we can give her a ride back to Prince George when we go in tomorrow."

"You are so good," I said. "We'll be right there."

Carol was grateful and happy to meet Johnny. I later learned that they had a long talk as Carol drank coffee and sobered up, and then had a good sleep, followed by another long talk in the morning before we left. Apparently, Carol recounted every detail of her time in my trailer and told Johnny everything, everything, even confessed that she wanted to "[make] a meal out of me and [come] back for more," quoting AC/DC, to which Johnny was thankfully oblivious.

Before we left Vermilion Lake that morning, Johnny called me close and said, "I love you Tom. You are a good man for me," and hugged me with all of her strength. "I love you too," I said. And inwardly I hoped that I was wrong in imagining that perhaps Carol was only the first of many women Dave had set up to show up at my doorstep. If that was true, it wouldn't be funny with Johnny in New York on the other side of the continent. And then I had a Gothic flash. Maybe Carol was a succubus after all, the first of a series of succubi that would be knocking on my door during the night, or dissolving through my trailer walls while Dave's ghost peered through the window smirking. But that seemed a bit ridiculous.

Hardly even noticing me or the scenery, Carol and Johnny talked and laughed like the best of new friends all the way to Prince George. They seemed oddly energized by each other. Carol told Johnny that her favorite song was "Bad Girlfriend" by Theory of a Dead Man, and Johnny responded by saying her favorite song was "Sicut Cervus" by Palestrina. They thought it was hysterical that they hadn't even heard of each other's favorite songs. (I hadn't heard of Johnny's.) Carol had put all of her clothes in a small plastic bag, and in the morning sun she looked transformed in the light blue summer dress Johnny had given to her, not leant to her. Johnny had also brushed Carol's hair for her and fixed it into a loose bun. The blue dress matched her eyes, and the blonde loose strands of her hair looked pretty. She wasn't wearing her heart-shaped medallion.

They really hit it off, and when we dropped off Carol at her apartment, Johnny got all of her info so they could stay in touch. Once Carol was home, we decided to get some lunch at Subway because Mass wasn't until 4:30 p.m., and Johnny's flight was not until 7:00 p.m.

As we were driving, Johnny said, "Carol has a lot going on in her soul, Tom. She told me last night that she is an only child of super-rigid scientific parents. Her dad is a research scientist with a PhD in Biology, and her mom has a PhD in Chemistry. Carol was forced to take classical piano lessons from the time she was five. Can you imagine? She told me she can play Frederic Chopin's Polonaise-fantaisie in A-flat major, Op. 61. Can you believe that? That piece is one of the most difficult pieces in the history of music. I didn't believe her until she used advanced music theory to explain the harmonic complexity of the piece. Listening to her was like listening to a physics lecture."

"A physics lecture?"

"Yeah. And in her teens, she dreamt of being a fashion designer, but her parents would only fund a pre-med program in science. Then she fell in love with a gifted young pianist named Vincenzo who broke her heart. Don't laugh, because she sure didn't laugh when she told me, but he dumped her and ran into the arms of a young violin prodigy named Natasha. Then Carol's life became a rockslide, everything was crumbling out of control and she left home and ended up working long hours for low wages just to pay for rent, and for a release she found herself sweating and wiggling in short-short jean cutoffs on country dance floors and falling for players like Dave who would show her at least some form of love, albeit ephemeral."

"Damn," I said. "I never would have guessed all that from what happened at my trailer last night."

"Carol is such a sweetheart. I'm definitely going to stay in touch with her."

At Subway, I ordered a foot-long meatball marinara, heavy on the mayo and black olives, with a large chocolate milk to wash it down, and to my surprise, Johnny said to the girl behind the glass, "I'll have the same as him, please." She smiled and snuggled up and put her arm through mine and said, "I want to see if we have the same taste buds."

We took our order to a booth and unwrapped our sandwiches and began eating. I was curious to see how Johnny was going to navigate her massive sub. How does an elegant, educated woman looking fresh after a good and interesting night's sleep—with a light coating of cherry lip balm on her firm lips—try to eat a saucy sandwich as thick as a small fence post? She lifted it into place and then smiled at me and said, "Here goes." Then she opened wide—her lips stretched open showing her perfectly clean and symmetrical teeth in welcoming rows—the meatballs and sauce were showing at the edges of the Italian bread and ready to ooze out at the slightest mishandling. Her fingers were applying a uniform Log Loader-like grip on the bread as her biting motion started to press down, and then she bit down firmly cutting through the end of the small loaf without any dripping or meatball spurting out and held the bun firmly and moved it away and down and smiled with a full mouth chewing. Absolutely gorgeous. I watched in a state of wonder, smiling. And as soon as her chewing allowed, she said cutely, "What?"

To which I replied, "You are gorgeous. I love the way you eat."

"My crazy boy," she said and took another bite demonstrating the same mastery of technique, although this time a bit of sauce oozed out, but she caught it in time and licked it before it dripped.

I basically attacked my sandwich. Just wolfed it down and washed back the chocolate milk in a few minutes without talking or whatever. Then I sat back ready to talk while Johnny was trying to finish hers, but she couldn't. She only ate a third of it and drank most of her milk and said she was stuffed, and she was sorry to waste the food, could I eat it? But I was stuffed too, so we just wrapped it up and talked for a while.

"That was good," she said. "Really delicious and filling."

"Yeah. That's my favorite. Do we have the same taste buds?"

"It looks like we are a match, Mr. Tems."

She sensed a speck of sauce on her bottom lip and wiped her mouth with napkins and then applied another light coating of cherry lip balm.

"I'm so glad I flew out to see you, Tom. It was a huge step forward for us, wasn't it? It's good to be together in person. It's so different from a distance"

"It was definitely interesting," I said. "Our map combined with meeting Carol made for quite a weekend."

She smiled at me with a look of understanding, as if she was starting to understand how I worked as a man. Then her green eyes seemed to dilate and the personal look she gave me made me feel like I was in her crosshairs and that she was breathing in a slow rhythm and about to squeeze off a shot.

Then she said, "Carol told me everything last night. It was a sign from God to hear you were able to resist her. You're a saint, Tom."

"A sign from God? I'm not sure I know what a saint really is, Johnny, but did Carol tell you how close I came to falling?" I said, genuinely embarrassed.

"Of course. But you're a healthy man and Carol is so attractive," and she reached over and held my hand firmly and looked fully into my eyes with her clear green eyes and said, "But you didn't want to fall, Tom. That's the point. You chose to be loyal. You fought for me."

I lowered my eyes in shame at how close I had come to blocking out Johnny and letting my animal hunger take control with Carol, and then Johnny reached for my jawline and gently lifted my face upwards and waited for eye contact and then said firmly to me, "You fought for me, Tom," and then she smiled widely, "Sounds medieval, doesn't it?"

My heart suddenly struck down pure white roots, deep roots rushing into blackish moist rich soil and spreading outwards into a lace-like expanding network of increasingly fine root hairs absorbing the moisture of her presence, and I smiled the smile of an understood man who is loved. And the time was right to kiss. And I felt her crosshairs on my face sawing slowly up and down with the rhythm of her breath and then resting on the target of my lips and we stood up out of our booth and there oblivious to the other customers concentrating on their sandwiches we held each other and pressed our lips together in an act of love. As her mouth hovered about to press, I sensed a few crumbs on my lips and on hers and I could smell the meatball sauce, we both could, and we smiled and said simultaneously without rehearsal, "You smell delicious," and then we touched our mouths together and then pressed and kissed fully and hugged tightly and then pulled back our faces while still embracing and simultaneously said, "I love you," and smiled, and then not just the exterior wall of the Subway and all of its windows, but also the entire parking lot, and half a block of the adjacent mall was blown into the sky like the 45 degree angle that blew out of the side of Mount St. Helens on May 18, 1980. Then we sat back down in the booth and looked at each other satisfied.

After that, we discussed Sally's condition and the strange feeling of her not seeing me, and of the emergence of our new love, and of the mystery of how time builds up and tears down and reconstructs the hearts of us all. It was beautiful and deep. But there was a gap between us. Our love was just now freshly building and I hadn't said anything about Sally's past kisses recalled at every detonation during the seven years blasting our path into the lake now recently recalled at every accurate shot I had recently fired. And as I sat smiling contentedly at Johnny there, I remembered my old Geography professor who had said that the blast area of Mount St. Helens had been left alone, no reclamation was planned, and the area was considered a kind of natural barren laboratory where scientists could observe regeneration working on its own natural terms without human intervention. And the analogy seemed solid, because there would be no reclamation of Sally—she was blasted into dust, and my mind was the barren expanse awaiting regeneration, and with Johnny's arrival there seemed to be signs of life pushing through the ash.

I guess my face indicated my reflections and Johnny asked, "What are you thinking, Tom. You look like you are somewhere else."

And I replied, "No, I am definitely here with you."

To which she replied with a smile, "Good. We should get to Sacred Heart Parish for Mass. It starts in 30 minutes. Are you okay with that? I never miss Sunday Mass."

"Absolutely."

As we drove, Johnny explained that we'd sit at the back and I should just observe. I should stand and sit when she and the congregation stood and sat, but I shouldn't kneel when they knelt. I should just sit at those times because kneeling would be inappropriate if I didn't "actually believe."

The church building was a modern design with a huge expanse of clear windows set in a high vaulted A-Frame. I watched Johnny cross herself with some holy water as we entered, and then we sat at the back as planned. Inside the church there was an array of modern religious art and what Johnny later described as The Stations of the Cross. The Latin Mass I was about to experience seemed absolutely medieval to me. It was a long and complex service punctuated with lots of old music, Gregorian chant, and polyphonic pieces. When we got to what's called the sign of peace, which is where you shake hands with those around you and say, "Peace be with you," Johnny took my hand but didn't shake it. She just held it and pulled me close and gave me a chaste kiss on the cheek and said, "Peace be with you, Tom." She looked at me as if we were married and she was pregnant with our first child. Later she explained that engaged and married couples kissed this way during the sign of peace, but no one else.

When it was time for communion, Johnny kindly whispered that I could come up for a blessing, but I should not take communion because I was not Catholic, or equally fine, I could just remain seated and wait for her to return. I said I'd just wait and observe, and she smiled and said, "Okay." Just as it was time for her to stand and join the line towards the front of the church, the polyphony choir began a piece with an ethereal introduction that seemed like an angelic weaving of male and female voices, and Johnny held my hand firmly and surprised said, "This is my favorite piece, 'Sicut Cervus,'" and smiled. Then she joined the line moving forward.

With her graceful back to me and her long red hair in an elegant pony tail vibrant in the light entering from the upper church windows and slanting down at us, and her motion under her modest white summer dress, Johnny drifted further down the aisle away from me. Then the light slanting down caught the emerald broach holding her hair and for a moment flashed a sharp green sparkle and then shifted to her shoulders and glowed there. Then she moved onwards and knelt at the communion rail and received a circular pure white wafer and then returned back towards me, her beautiful head downwards in contemplation. And then she silently moved next to me in the pew and then onto her knees in prayer on the kneeler for a few minutes in silence while I watched the whole scene around me.

Then she moved back into the pew next to me and held my hand and looked lovingly into my eyes and said, "I love you, Tom. Thanks for coming with me." "No problem," I said and smiled.

As we drove to the airport I told her that her favorite song was brilliant, and it fit her personality perfectly. "How so," she asked, and I said, "I couldn't understand the Latin words, but just the sound of it seemed to be an inspired weaving of passion and order, energy and finely rendered detail."

She smiled and translated the Psalm that Palestrina used as his text. It describes a deer thirsting in the desert, thirsting for a fresh stream of water, and "that stream symbolizes God."

"That's awesome," I said, and inwardly I thought of my thirst for Johnny and how she was becoming the stream in my barren landscape.

Then I visualized the verdant strip of foliage along the artery of Windhover Creek beyond my range and its entrance into Vermilion Lake and then its exit down and away from the lake like fresh life leaving the lake behind with gravity flowing towards the ocean far out of sight in the distance.

And then I had a bizarre flash and visualized a huge flat TV screen with two You Tube videos playing side by side simultaneously, on the left side was Carol's favorite song "Bad Girlfriend" booming at high volume in a strip bar pulsating with sweaty stoned youth, and on the right side was a New York City St.

Patrick's Cathedral concert performance of "Sicut Cervus" at moderate volume with a formally dressed audience attentive to every musical nuance. And I reflected on the miracle of how such a piece could trace itself back through countless millennia to the big bang that started it all.

I burst out laughing and Johnny said, "What?" and I responded, "I was just thinking about you and Carol. What a pair."

"She's a wonderful young woman, Tom. She is so thirsty for love. She's been in a desert all her life. I'll be praying for her and staying in touch. I'm certain that God has a remarkable plan for her life."

I just smiled and absorbed Johnny. There was not even a fiber of judgement in her. There seemed to be no brakes now. My heart was like a boulder that had been blasted into the sky and was now helpless against gravity. All I could do was brace myself and see where it would come to rest.

We arrived at the airport around 6:00 p.m. The sky was bright blue and streaked with thin ribbons of cloud moving slowly across the skyline. Based on the current wind, it looked like the sky would be vacant of all cloud by the time Johnny's plane lifted off. I flinched at the thought of her not being within reach, of her being out of sight and distant again. That pattern seemed to be the heart of my entire adult life. I would watch her dissolve into the blue distance like a dream. We took care of her baggage and then found a seat close to the boarding tunnel. She explained her current plans for work and her schedule with Sally and the reconstruction of her memories. The psychologist had outlined three distinct theories for Johnny to experiment with, and she was to record any sparks of recovered memory in a journal.

She would call me regularly using Skype and then visit again in person during the last weekend in August.

"What do you have in mind for the next three weeks, besides dreaming about me?" she asked.

I smiled and explained, "First, I'm going to reload a batch of the most accurate load I recently tested. Then I'll be shooting at my range on Saturdays and Sundays every weekend until I see you again."

"Watch out for grizzlies."

"I'll have my gun back there, don't worry."

When the call to board the plane was announced, it was hard to let each other go. And when we kissed one last time and had to stop touching and space seemed to flood in between us like a landslide that couldn't be resisted because if she didn't physically move down the tunnel and leave the plane would leave without her, she looked at me like she did when we exchanged the sign of peace at Mass earlier that day. It was as if she was a genuinely happy new bride and growing within her was our first child. I felt solid inside as she turned in the tunnel and disappeared. At the departure window, I held up my hand and waved slowly skyward as her plane roared and then lifted off into the blank blue sky, clean and cloudless and endless, and her plane became increasingly small until it became a speck and then dissolved.

CHAPTER EIGHTEEN:

Work was slow on Monday morning, and I had time to think about the world Johnny lived in, the ideas and hopes expressed at the Mass, and how for her eternity seemed to be mysteriously obvious in time and everything around us. I thought about how marriage and conception had cosmic significance to her, how she believed they were a big deal. They weren't to the people I knew in the 21st century.

That day I treated a few minor cuts towards noon, but around 2:00 p.m. I had to deal with a serious Straddle Injury. Wain Burns, a young framing carpenter working on the west side of the lake, had fallen from a roof and straddled a beam on his way down. His testicles were smashed to hell and he was in agony. When they rushed him into my first-aid station, his face was contorted and all of his limbs were trembling. I gave him the strongest painkiller I'm allowed to keep at the station and had him ambulanced to the emergency ward in Prince George. There was no question he had internal bleeding that would require a specialist's assessment. The rest of my shift was quiet.

That night around 9:00 p.m. there was a light knock on my trailer door, followed by a series of slightly more confident knocks. At first I thought it might be someone from work with an update on Wain, but when I went to the window, there, brightly lit in my porch light was Carol, sober, smiling, alert, and well dressed in a light yellow flowing summer dress with a square neckline. She was wearing only a hint of makeup and her blonde hair was clean and glossy and up in a messy bun, and around her neck she wore a short string of pinkish pearls. On her feet were light yellow wedge dress shoes. Her toenails were painted black and they looked delicately stark in her shoes.

When I opened the door, she smiled widely and her teeth were perfectly clean and white and her facial bone structure was strikingly elegant. It was hard to believe she was the same woman I had first met drunk and disoriented. Obviously, something had changed since she had met Johnny. Her sober voice was very different. She sounded much smarter, and her enunciation was almost amusingly crisp — the opposite of the slurring young woman Dave had posthumously sent my way.

"Please come in, Carol. I'm surprised to see you. You look really healthy. You look great."

"Johnny's a good motivator. She's got more going for her mind and body than any woman I've ever known. You are such a lucky man, Tom."

Carol paused, and then said, "She told me a bit about your difficulties as a child. I hope you don't mind?"

"Not at all. I was a kid then. That's ancient history now."

There was a brief silence, and then I said, "Johnny was excited about your music. I never would have guessed that, Carol."

"You're not alone. No guy has ever guessed it. But it's part of me. It's actually the one meaningful thing I've been able to salvage out of my childhood."

"It is meaningful," I said, "and it's strange that you should drop by tonight because after work today I listened to the Chopin piece Johnny mentioned. In fact, I listened to it carefully twice. This will probably sound stupid because I'm a barbarian when it comes to complex music, but the more I listened to it the more it sounded simple to play. It seemed as natural and simple as a flower opening."

"It is natural and simple, Tom."

Carol looked at me and smiled slightly as if she was pleased with our discussion but wanted to head in a very different direction. She asked if we could sit and talk, and I said of course. We sat at either end of the couch facing each other. She adjusted her dress so as to cover as much of her knees as the fabric would allow, and with her feet aligned towards me, she began what she really came for.

"Tom, I assume that Johnny has shared everything we have talked about with you, but I've come here tonight to speak privately, honestly, and privately. If you'd like me to leave right now I will, but if I stay and express myself I need you to promise that what we discuss will never be shared with Johnny or anyone else. This isn't about secrets or infidelity or behind other people's backs or betraying friends, this is about adults being honest and private, no more. I want to remain friends with Johnny. She's incredible. But if you can agree to my privacy requirement there is something I'd really like you to know. If not, then that something will have to dissolve unspoken and this visit is over now. Can you agree that our discussion will remain private?"

I stood up and paced towards the kitchen and got a beer and asked Carol if she wanted one and she said maybe later. I cracked mine and took a drink and said, "What you're asking makes me really uncomfortable, Carol. You need to give me some sort of framework before I can answer you. You are asking me to keep something secret from Johnny. That isn't right no matter how you phrase it."

"I want to discuss your future happiness, Tom."

"Are you suggesting there is something about Johnny that I should know? Something she hasn't or wouldn't ever tell me?"

"I can't say more unless I have your guarantee of privacy, Tom."

"And if I were to phone Johnny right now and explain what you are asking of me, what do you think she'd say?"

"I think she'd want to talk to me in private, and I'd tell her that if she could promise me privacy that I'd be happy to share my thoughts with her too. I'd offer her the same option as I'm offering you. But I don't think you want to call her, because you would never know what you had missed, and I'd be gone forever."

Carol stood up and adjusted her dress so that the light yellow cotton flowed over her ribs and then loosened slightly as it curved over her hips and towards her knees as it was designed to do. Her blue eyes were fixed on me and her face was lovely but serious as she waited for my reply.

"I can't decide. Fuck it, I guess you better leave."

"Nothing bad, Tom, just my honest feelings."

"Honest feelings about what?"

"All I can say is what I've already said. I want to discuss your future happiness."

I'd had enough of her bullshit. "Okay, damn it, you've got your promise of privacy."

"Thank you, Tom. Please sit down and relax. Like I said, it's nothing bad."

Once Carol had sat down too, I said, "Let's have it then."

"I just want you to have a choice, Tom. From the first moment that I met you I felt a deep connection. I know I came on too fast and strong, but that's behind me now. My mind is clear. I've been thinking about you constantly and for a moment please don't get angry and let me present you with two options."

"Two options? I'm happy now. What is there to choose?"

"Johnny is a brilliant and beautiful religious woman. I could never compete with her intelligence. But I have music, and you have to admit I am lovely. I know you think so. It's obvious when you look at me. Johnny has ideals she calls medieval. She's told me about them, and they are the stuff of storybook fantasy, complete with no premarital sex, a huge church wedding, and the love of God involved in everything ever after."

"You came here to insult her?"

"I certainly did not, Tom. I just want to offer you an option. Johnny has confided in me that her faith involves certain restrictions, what she calls tapping the brakes slightly at a few dangerous corners. Has she mentioned this to you?"

"She has, and I'm fine with her boundaries, and they are no business of yours."

"Please don't be angry, as I said, I just want you to know something. I want you to know that if you were to choose me, I would never put you behind bars or fence you in with razor wire or post armed guards."

"What are you saying?"

"You would not have to commit to me in marriage. You would not have to struggle to support a growing family, and you would never have to endure any tapping of brakes on dangerous corners."

"Choose you? I don't even know you, Carol."

"Please hear me out, Tom. I don't have brakes, and I love dangerous corners. I'll never forget the look on your face and your reaction when you read the inscription on my medallion. Your mouth was dry and you were hard. I know what you want. And you need to know that Johnny has told me in no uncertain terms that as her husband you will never receive that pleasure from her. That is a big tap on a dangerous corner. You'll be married for life and never even once be able to relax and have your cock properly sucked and your honey swallowed, not dutifully gagged down, but deliciously swallowed and savored as yummy. I'd never put you through that kind of bleak starvation, Tom. Choose me, and I'll happily suck you off and swallow whenever you want me to. That's a promise. Keep this as my guarantee."

And then she handed me her heart-shaped medallion.

"Are you fucking crazy, Carol, coming here and talking to me like that?"

"Please don't be angry. I'm being honest, Tom. Think about what I said. You don't believe in her religion and neither do I. That's the truth. We could have a lot of fun together."

"I think you better leave now, Carol."

"Of course, Tom. I understand that I've shocked you. When you are alone in bed tonight, think about what I've told you. I've been honest."

Carol stood up and adjusted her dress and smiled, and then she walked out my front door and left it open behind her. I walked out onto the porch and watched her leave. The street lights glazed her as she passed under them. And as she walked up the sidewalk to her small white car, her hips moved softly from side to side as her smooth muscles moved under her cotton dress. As her honest words dissolved into silence, the motion of her arms and thighs and the way she held her head and then her pretty face looking back at me as she waved all seemed pure in a strange way, and everything about her seemed as natural and simple as a flower. I gripped her medallion firmly as her vehicle pulled away and moved down my street and then turned and disappeared. Then I shoved the medallion into the right front pocket of my jeans.

Then I went back into my trailer and sat at the kitchen table. I drank my beer in silence as I finished up some cartons of Mexican food from the weekend. Then I brushed my teeth, shut off all of the lights, and lay down on my bed.

"A slider down and away. Carol could make a fortune in the big leagues," I said aloud as I looked upwards into the darkness. "How the hell am I supposed to swing at a pitch like that?"

Then in the darkness I started to fade away and then I slept deeply. The dimmer switch was rotated slowly and the yellowish lights of a prison visiting area faintly emerged and then the fluorescent lights were bright and their ballasts hummed. I was the only visitor seated in a chair in a slot-like walled compartment facing a thick plate glass window and a gray concrete wall with a massive reinforced blue metal door encrusted with locks across and ten yards down from me on the prisoners' side to the right. A heavy, bouncer-like guard with a crew cut and an expressionless face came into view and unlocked the door and let Sally enter the hall and directed her to the chair across from me. She looked through the plate glass and seemed puzzled.

"Why have you brought me here? There's no one here," she said as she turned to the guard. Then she looked through me again and repeated, "There's no one here."

I looked at the guard and he was opening the door again—turning the heavy key, and a thin grayish shadow of Dave entered the hallway. He looked at me and smiled and said, "Finally, a fucking visitor. How are you doing, man?" As Dave was about to sit down across from me, he crumbled and vanished and the guard loudly called to me, "Who are you waiting for, anyway?" Then he locked the door and walked down the concrete hall to the right and out of view and the dimmer switch turned down to pitch-black.

Then the lights above me hummed and slowly brightened again, and in front of me was the inmate I had come to visit. He was a heavily tattooed large man with a shaved head and intense blue eyes. He was expressionless and rigid, and both of his arms—one fully sleeved in blue designs, the other fully sleeved in green designs—were alive. Then almost machine-like he slowly pressed his palms hard and flat against the security glass.

"What the hell are you doing?" the guard called out.

The prisoner's eyes dilated, and then flickered and motioned me to look at his palms. Through the glass I tried to read the tattooed script. There was a single word carved—it seemed—into each palm, perhaps a name. Then the power in my trailer failed and I heard my fridge rattle and make a loud crunching sound and I woke up to my alarm clock blinking at 3:39 a.m. The power was out. Then I heard the backup generator kick in and then the lights surged back on.

CHAPTER NINETEEN:

Tuesday morning at work I learned that there had been rockslides in back of the mountains near my range site on the weekend. Will New came into my first-aid station at 9:00 a.m. He seemed very different. He smelled of whisky and wanted to talk to me. His words were slurred. He said the turbulence happened in two waves: on Saturday night and then early Sunday morning. The first mild tremor and slide happened around 8:30 p.m. on Saturday night, and then the second more aggressive tremor and slide around 2:30 a.m. on Sunday morning. As if trying to pry something out of me, he asked if Johnny (he referred to her as Ms. Nostal) had ever mentioned anything about how her design might be linked to the tremors, and I asked him what he meant by linked.

He claimed that when Ms. Nostal originally presented her plans to the development committee, she put forward her conception of the project as a kind of romantic Bermuda Triangle, and that she was detailed in her explanation of how the design would work, and that she had kept them guessing as to whether she was speaking literally or invoking a fantasy scenario as an advertising ploy to attract the romantically challenged. Will said her responses were suspiciously evasive, and in his opinion, she'd conjured the project into production. She'd charmed the committee members into a sleepy haze. But now they were "waking up."

Waking up? Brain-dead idiots, I thought to myself. Will was insulting Johnny's intelligence and heart, and so I was straight.

"Did it ever occur to your committee that her plan was a metaphor for the turbulence and accidents of the heart? What if being lost at sea and storms symbolize a time of prelude, after which the calm of true love arrives? Obviously there are no poets on your committee, Will. How can you build without imagination? And what do you mean by romantically challenged?"

Will babbled back, "All of the wealthy are romantically challenged. They are the people who realize they are aging fast and that probably sooner than later they will be in a box 8 feet under forever. When it's too late, they realize they've lost their shot at true love."

Then Will raised his arms into a stance of violent universal embrace and yelled, "They realize their past lovers have not been lovers at all, but rather the beautiful poor faking for cash. The beautiful poor!"

Then he lowered his arms and clenched both fists and venomously slurred, "These rich sons of bitches are the romantics who will bite the bait that Ms. Nostal's project dangles."

To which I fired back: "You better talk to Ms. Nostal yourself, Will. What you're implying is poisonous. Obviously you don't know her. And what do you mean by tremors and slides being 'linked' to her design? Is that some more twisted speculation?"

"We're beginning to see the occult at work here, Tom."

"The occult! You stink of booze, Will. You're out of your mind."

"She's a medieval witch, Tom. She's probably been alive for centuries. I can see it in her eyes."

"You're crazy, Will. You're literally nuts! What the fuck has gotten into you? I'm reporting you to the committee. I hope to hell you don't own a gun. You're a dangerous fuck now."

"Fuck you, Tom!" he yelled, and then he tried to swagger out of my first-aid station. He was on the verge of staggering, but didn't. He was just sober enough to walk straight out of my sight.

"What the hell was that all about?" I said aloud.

I called Sam Mayco, the senior project manager, as soon as Will was down the stairs and gone, and he said the committee was aware that Will had just recently started drinking.

"We're sorry he came over and bothered you, Tom."

"I don't care about me, Sam. I care that his insane ravings are contaminating the beauty and intelligence of Johnny's plans."

"What insane ravings?" he asked.

"It doesn't matter. He was drunk," I said.

If Will had been bullshitting me about the committee and they hadn't heard his contamination yet, I wasn't going to spread it. Let it die.

Sam explained, "Will's wife, Brandy, left him a week ago and after calling her continuously, trying to get back with her, she finally picked up and told him it was over, they were dead, and he took it hard."

"Apparently, Will bought a case of Canadian Club whisky when she first fucked off," Sam went on, "but he didn't plan to open the case unless it really was over. It looks like he's opened it."

"Yeah, and it doesn't look like the booze is solving much," I said.

"Never has, never does," Sam said. "We'll reel him in and sober him up, don't worry, Tom."

"Sounds good," I said and hung up.

At Sam's prompting, the committee called Will's wife that same afternoon and let her know the condition he was in, and they pleaded with her to try to get back with Will. They really needed him as head of the surveying crew. His drunkenness was costing them a fortune in lost productivity. Brandy said, "No way. We are done." But they offered to pay her $100,000 cash to take a single boat ride with Will into the center of Vermilion Lake that evening at sunset, stay there floating for 15 minutes, and then return to shore. They said if she felt the same way once they docked, then they'd not trouble her again and they'd accept that it was over. That was a lot of cash, so she agreed. Will had no idea about the money; he thought it was her idea, and he was eager and showered and drank a lot of coffee. They rowed out into the lake, floated there, and then returned. And after they docked the committee was happy to see that they were arm in arm and laughing.

The next morning Will came into my first-aid station and asked me if I had anything he could rub onto his lower spine, the lumbar region, because he had nearly thrown out his back while he and Brandy were making up the previous night. He was smiling from ear to ear and as sober as a judge and looked very healthy. His skin was glowing and obviously his circulation was in good shape.

"Ms. Nostal is a genius, Tom. Please forgive and forget the filth I spoke yesterday. To be honest, I am violently allergic to alcohol. It's like I'm a character in a horror movie when I fall off the wagon. I've not done that in 20 years. Please forgive me."

"Absolutely, Will. We're human, not stainless steel robots."

"It was like our wedding night, Tom. I couldn't believe it. Everything about her was fresh and clean and we just did each other like there was no tomorrow, almost broke the bed frame. Ms. Nostal is a genius."

"She is something else. That's for certain, Will."

And I gave him some of the heavy duty stuff for serious lovers: Wild Horse Liniment for Romantics. He shook my hand firmly and walked out with a swagger, slightly favoring his back as he walked, proud of his injury and his bottle of stallion rub.

The week had gotten off to an interesting start, for sure, and when Johnny called me on Friday night it became a massive rockslide. She said that on Monday night, Sally hit her with a deluge of memories and revelations of past events, a literal torrent of autobiography pouring out of her. Sally couldn't sleep and she kept Johnny up all night with her recollections. She said the tidal wave was still flowing. The large brush strokes and all of the main events had rushed back to Sally, and now she was experiencing waves of minutia—nuanced details of crystal clear scenes from the past and even every detail of the accident and her hospital experiences in Prince George, meeting Dave, and meeting me for the first time in the hospital when we came to visit.

"But she can't remember why the accident happened, Tom. Why she was in that rough back country in the first place," Johnny said. "And yet, she remembers why she had the large statue of Our Lady of Mount Carmel lodged behind her driver's seat—she was bringing it to Sister Angelica as a gift for the hermitage."

Johnny explained that Sally's faith had suddenly returned. She said, "It's as if her faith has been reinserted during an operation. Sally is now convinced that God is calling her to a contemplative life."

Also, Sally didn't understand why Johnny was shocked. She had no memory of Johnny's recent attempts to catechize her, but she fully remembered her mom and dad and their spirituality and family events and racing and Motown and deer hunting with her dad, and her dad's death at the racetrack, and Mom moving to South Bend while they attended The University of Notre Dame, and all of her Drama classes and professors and acting coaches, and everything else right up to the present. Everything except me prior to the accident.

Johnny said she carefully probed Sally as she was recalling complex full-length accounts of her recent and distant past, and wherever I had once played a central or even a peripheral role, her mind had excised my character and, as Johnny put it, "stitched up any loose tissue as if her subconscious were performing emergency reconstructive surgery." She didn't call earlier in the week because she was in shock and wanted to hear the doctor's opinion first.

The doctor was surprised when Johnny and Sally came into his office and he evaluated her. He later explained to Johnny in private, to avoid further confusing Sally, that in very rare cases memories lost through intense physical trauma can suddenly become reinstated, but he'd never seen a case where a particular person had been removed from a patient's life history, as in Sally's case with me. Sally's case was unique, he said. The doctor asked Johnny to conduct an experiment and gently inquire about other boys Sally might have known during adolescence, dated as a teen, and so forth, just to check if all male relationships had been deleted. The doctor had some theory in mind. But when Johnny did this over a few days, Sally happily discussed her past boyfriends, all of whom were described by her as semi-shy chaste Catholic boys, and all of whom her dad had firmly cautioned to respect Sally. Roman had inspired this respect by first showing each suitor his gun collection and then invoking the Holy Trinity while waving an incense burner over the suitor before he left on his date with

Sally. Thick clouds of fragrant smoke would cling to each of these boys as they walked Sally to the bus stop to go to the movies or skating at the local rink.

"She has no memory of you, Tom, the love of her life. You have vanished. I can only assume that the Lord has a plan in all this."

And Sally was stunned to learn that Dave had died, and she was offering prayers for him daily.

I listened to all of this in amazement. It was a huge shift and clearing of the air. Sally was back, and she was going full tilt towards becoming a sister in a contemplative order. Sally was motivated and energetic and back to where she was before the accident at the lake, and I was permanently out of the picture. As I watched Johnny's face on Skype as she blasted me with all of this new information on Friday night, it was clear that she was relieved—the weight of an uncertain future had been lifted from her shoulders.

Her expression told me that it was safe to land, and so I did. I said, "Johnny," and paused to get her full attention. Then when she was looking straight into her computer's webcam at me, I said, "This may seem sudden, and I know that I'm not an internationally known target shooter yet, but I am crazy in love with you. Will you marry me?"

She stared back neutrally, so I jumped in with, "I know I'm not Catholic, and I can't promise I ever will be, not because of any negative vibes but just because I'm mystified and I can't profess a faith I really don't understand yet or maybe never will, but I am open to it and I am contemplating what I'm learning, and I would totally support raising our kids in the faith like you said ... "

And then she cut me off with a squeal of joy, "Yes, yes, yes, Tom, I just want to kiss you, yes, yes, yes, yes. I accept. But our wedding must be medieval, Tom. Please don't think I'm being difficult, but it must be. It will be all in Latin, with Gregorian chant, and with polyphony. We'll have to register in a marriage preparation course, get a license, talk to the priest, coordinate the choirs, ... "

And then it was my turn to cut her off, "Thank you for saying yes, Johnny. I love you and I won't let you down. Just relax and tell me our next step."

She told me the easy first step was for me to buy us a marriage license in Prince George. The second step was to visit the priest at Sacred Heart Parish to sign us up for a marriage course, but it would have to be offered on consecutive weekends.

"Then we'll talk to the father about a date for our solemn engagement ceremony, ideally in about two months, and then have the actual wedding in a little over a year. We don't have to fix an exact date now, but we can expect the wedding will not be more than 18 months after our solemn engagement service. How does that sound?"

"It sounds like you know what you are doing. This weekend I'll shoot, and then next week I'll take a day off to get the license and talk to the priest. Okay?"

"I love you, Tom. You've made me so happy. Our future is going to be so good."

Johnny was glowing with joy and so was I. It was the best night of my life. I felt connected, deep, solid. We said good night; then I showered and crashed. I wanted to reload in the morning, and I needed to be well rested and focused.

CHAPTER TWENTY:

My alarm went off at 9:00 a.m. and I jumped out of bed eager to have a good breakfast and start reloading. I've always loved reloading. The precision and ritual culminating in squeezing off the shot, the whole process fascinates me. That Saturday morning after breakfast and a large strong coffee to keep me alert, I prepared my reloading bench. First, I dusted and cleared the area; then I opened my gun safe and got my powder and projectiles. I was going to make up sixty rounds of the most accurate load from my previous visit to the range, which was 100.0 grains of H 1000 combined with a Prov 271 magnum primer and the 250 grain Sierra BTHP MatchKing bullet, and all in a COR brass case with a C.O.L. of 3.681. This combination had tested as incredible, and I was hoping to see those results repeated again.

All shooters know that there are numerous variables at work in any accuracy test: wind, heat, condition of the shooter, and a deluge of concentration and technique issues. And my mentor, Jake Wardelle, had taught me to be machine-like in technique and repeat the exact muscular and breath-related patterns with the identical mental imagery for each shot. And it was this latter element that had disturbed my last session at the range. Visualizing Sally's mouth versus Johnny's mouth had played no small part in my final results, and today I was determined to focus only on Johnny's mouth. We were getting married, and no woman other than Johnny—regardless of context—had any place in my imagination.

With this resolution in mind, I set up and bolted into place my powder measure and set up my powder scale. Some shooters might think my equipment primitive and out of date compared to the most modern electronic scales and accessories, but I preferred then, and still do now, to work more slowly and carefully with simpler technology and measure and weigh each powder charge and seat each bullet by hand, rotating the case once the bullet is halfway into the case neck and then pressing it all the way home with a second repetition of the lever. I have always loved my RCBS full-length resizing and bullet-seating dies. They've always worked perfectly for me, but I have especially loved them since finding Johnny. Because all RCBS products either come in green plastic boxes (like their resizing and bullet-seating dies), or have bright green handles (like their primer pocket brushes), or are an opaque green (like their metallic case trays), or are a luminous, transparent bright green (like their powder measures), their products remind me of Johnny's eyes. That may sound a bit odd, but it's true.

That morning I filled my powder measure, prepared and leveled my scale, and filled my Lee Auto-Prime with Prov 271 magnum primers. Before priming the cases, I conducted my usual distraction prevention ritual. I went into the living room and made sure my front door was locked and switched off all of the lights and set the landline phone to zero ringtone. Then I pulled closed my bedroom door and locked it—even though I was alone in my trailer—and then I put on my safety goggles and began priming the cases. I seated the primers carefully and double-checked that they were fully seated and that none of them appeared to be too deeply seated, which is an indicator that the primer pocket has been reamed out too deeply and the case should be thrown away because the firing pin might not hit the primer with enough force to create a crisp ignition of the powder. With the large powder charges in a .338 Lapua Mag cartridge a crisp ignition is no minor matter. It didn't take long to prime the sixty cases and they all looked great and ready to charge.

When using a powder measure, it's crucial to hold the mouth of the case firmly against the base of the measure and then stroke the dispensing lever fully into its highest position to release the set charge, and then lower it smoothly and steadily to allow any final grains to trickle into the case before placing the case back into the reloading tray. And so I began, there in what Johnny would probably call a kind of profound monastic silence, lifting and lowering smoothly, rhythmically, like a carefully adjusted machine, rhythmically and smoothly lifting and lowering, and as I relaxed into that focused zone, I had a flash of our wedding night and Johnny first beneath me and then on top of me lifting and lowering her hips smoothly, rhythmically, like a carefully adjusted machine, rhythmically and smoothly lifting and lowering, and then I snapped out of it and said aloud, "What the hell? Clear your head, Tom. You're working with 60,000 pounds of pressure per square inch here. Wake the hell up." And so I did.

I splashed my face with a memory. I clearly recalled my surprise when Jake first described how much chamber pressure was next to my cheek as I pulled the trigger on a reload—between 55,000 to 60,000 pounds per square inch. And I also recalled my amazement that the bullet would exit the muzzle at 3,000 feet per second. I'll never forget how as I marveled at the physics of shooting, Jake said to me, "It's nothing to be surprised at, Tom. Like that bullet, you too would be moving at 3,000 feet per second if you had 60,000 pounds of pressure on your ass!" I smiled and continued working.

I had charged all but two of the sixty primed cases when my cell phone ringtone kicked in loud with Robert Palmer's "Simply Irresistible." I'd forgotten to shut the damn thing off. "Damn," I yelled and picked it up. It was Johnny.

She was bubbly and said in an endearing voice, "Good morning my handsome fiancé. How are you doing?"

"I'm doing great, 'sugar plum,'" I answered and laughed.

"Sugar plum?"

"Or 'baby doll,' or 'honeysuckle,' or just plain 'honey,' whichever you prefer now that we're engaged."

"Are you serious? If I have to choose, I'll pick 'sugar plum' for now, but in the future I'd really prefer 'my dear bride.'"

"Sounds good."

She was bursting with enthusiasm about our upcoming solemn engagement ceremony. It was obviously very important to her. As she went on and on (in a good way, flowing with excitement and relevant concerns and details, such as her mother Clara, in South Bend, Illinois, having to be there because it wouldn't be complete without her, and I've never even met her, and many other important emotions and considerations gushing at me as I stood there next to my serenely laid out reloading materials), it occurred to me that our solemn engagement was like a good target load: we'd have to resize and clean the brass, dry it carefully, prime the case, pour the powder, seat the bullet, and give it a final buffing with diaper flannel and it would be ready to fire. I kept this to myself, of course, as Johnny let her happiness flow, and I smiled. I was moved to see her so happy. And I thought of the first time I ever spoke to her in that Shelby at the car show during her first visit and how far we had come in so brief a time and here we were on the threshold of "until death do us part." Johnny had talked to me earlier about the vows she wanted if we ever married. She said the vows would have to demonstrate a commitment to the full medieval package: "For better, for worse, for richer, for poorer, in sickness and in health, until death do us part." And I said that was fine with me. She finally settled down and we talked like lovers for a while and agreed to talk again on Sunday night. She'd let me get back to my reloading.

I made sure my cell phone was turned off. I refocused, and got back to work. I finished charging the final two cases and I was ready to seat the bullets and get out to the range. If you've never seen a 250 grain Sierra Boat Tail Hollow Point MatchKing bullet, trust me, it is a thing of beauty, the absolute ultimate in aerodynamic efficiency. Bordering on "with reverence" I seated the sixty projectiles, polished each round to a high brilliance with baby blue diaper flannel, and then gently placed each round into my large green RCBS ammo boxes. Then I packed up my rifle and reloading bag and made a lunch and was ready to head out to the range.

The sun was hot and the sky was clear and there was no wind. It would be a great day for shooting. I had it made. I was engaged to an intelligent and absolutely beautiful woman who loved me, and hey, it may be a guy thing, but I had a super-accurate rifle that I loved and what's more, I had a dream of earning good money doing what I love, shooting long range. As I fired up the truck, I popped James Brown's greatest hits into the CD player and rolled out of there happy, blasting "I feel good ... so good, so good, I got you."

In about twenty minutes I was off road and behind the mountains. As I approached my range, I could see where the rockslides had come down. They were to the right of my line of sight about thirty yards from my shooting path and were of no concern to me. I planned to set up and fire forty rounds at two targets, grab some lunch, clean my rifle thoroughly, and then fire a final twenty rounds and call it a day. I laid out my shooting mat, spread on top of it my shooting blanket to keep any sand away from my ammo, and set up my spotting scope. These rounds would be shot from the standard prone position required in formal competitions, not from my Workmate bench like the previous rounds. Then I filled the magazine of my Sako TRG 42 rifle and threw the sling over my right shoulder, grabbed three targets and my stapler, and began my walk out to the plywood target boards.

The bear scat we saw earlier was dried and shrunken and I kept my eyes open for any sign of that grizzly as I walked. This time I had my loaded gun with me, so I was at peace. As I walked alone there along the back of those mountains, I thought of Vermilion Lake on the other side and Johnny's beautiful mind which had designed the entire project, and the caliber of the woman I was soon to marry really hit me. I was shooting for her, for our future, so that working together we could build a secure life for our family. Her dream was to be "a fruitful vine in our home," and she hoped to conceive many children who would be "like olive shoots around our table," she said. I remember thinking that this was an interesting analogy to be sure, but never having grown olives I was probably missing something important, I suspected. Nevertheless, I felt solid and grounded for the first time in my life. And I didn't want that feeling to ever leave.

By the time I reached the plywood, the sun was immediately overhead and the slight wind I first felt was completely stilled. I stapled the targets in place and took time to slowly sweep the entire area with my vision, checking for any grizzly sign. I noticed a white-headed eagle flying high in the sky ahead of me in the distance.

"That grizzly is probably foraging for roots and salal berries along the northern edge of Windhover

Creek," I said aloud as if someone were next to me. "I can't see any fresh tracks. It looks like we can shoot in peace."

As I walked back to my shooting mat, I mentally rehearsed the breathing and muscle patterns Jake had taught me as a young marksman, and I was excited to confirm that the load I had developed was my championship combination. But I also rehearsed my visualization of Johnny's perfect mouth, and all the way back to my line of fire I calmly repeated aloud these words, "The perfect mouth of 'my dear bride' is my delight ... fade to serene black ... eyes open ... pause ... breath ... slow squeeze ... BANG," and I visualized her in vivid photographic color smiling, and the light coating of cherry lip balm, and the perfect rows of her immaculate white teeth, and her pink clean tongue, and her slightly upturned upper lip, and I repeated aloud, "The beautiful lips of 'my dear bride' are my delight ... fade to the peace of night ... eyes open ... pause ... breath ... slow squeeze ... BANG," until I was back. Then I attached the tripod to my rifle and pulled on my snug leather shooting jacket, deep hunter green leather with light green inserts, and knelt down on my mat facing the distant targets at 1000 meters and got comfortable and ready to shoot. I removed my full magazine and popped in my empty second magazine.

Then I began with the target on the left, and loading a single cartridge at a time—leaving my bolt open between rounds to let my action cool, and checking the point of impact with my spotting scope for each shot fired, and timing my string of twenty rounds so that the heat of my heavy Sako barrel wouldn't influence my accuracy—within twenty minutes I had completed my first target. It was an impressive group by any standard, about the size of a grapefruit, but I had hoped for better. Often the first shots out of a cold clean barrel are flyers, that is, a bit wild, until the barrel is a bit dirtier and stabilized, and I hoped that was what caused the lower score.

Then it hit me that without thinking I had shot that string of twenty without thinking. I had dropped into a kind of Zen no mind and not thought of Johnny. So I let my rifle cool until the barrel was only slightly warm to the touch, and then squeezed off the second set of twenty rounds being careful to visualize Johnny's mouth as I had rehearsed. The difference in accuracy was remarkable. Through my spotting scope I could see that all twenty shots were contained in a circle no larger than a plum. It was impossible. I was pumped.

I let my rifle cool completely as I sat on the tailgate of the truck and breathed deeply and ate my lunch. In my cooler the ice rustled as I pulled out a large bottle of chocolate milk and a thick Swiss cheese, lettuce and tomato with heavy mayo sandwich on whole grain bread. I was hungry and feeling strong and wolfed the sandwich down and ate a banana and washed it all down with the chocolate milk. Then I placed my rifle in the cleaning vice in the box of my truck and gave it a thorough cleaning with powder solvent, then copper remover, then powder solvent again, and then multiple passes with patches soaked in WD 40. I felt really good about my gun. No doubt it's a guy thing, but providing for my family with my gun just had a solid kind of pioneer feel about it and I felt masculine, sweaty, strong, and ready to marry and please my wife with my strength.

As I knelt on my shooting mat and moved into prone position, I challenged myself to make these next twenty shots the best shots I had ever fired, perfectly held, visualized, squeezed off, calm follow-through, everything. It was beautiful. Each shot had a crisp bang and recoil that felt identical and precision machined. I was in a place I had never been as a shooter, a zone of perfection. The clean holes in the target at 1000 meters were within an inch of each other, and a few of them were touching.

By the time I got to round nineteen, I realized that I was on the verge of a world record score. It would never count, of course, because there was no witness and it was not a registered competition, but I would know the score was real, and that would be enough. As I carefully placed round nineteen into the action of my rifle and gently slid the bolt closed and pushed down the bolt handle securing the massive locking lugs in my Sako action, I thought of our upcoming wedding. Johnny and I would close the action on our love and detonate the force of our passion. I smiled, checked the wind flags, they were hanging limp in the windless path to the target in the distance, and visualized Johnny's smile as I breathed slowly in and out, sawing smoothly, vertically through the center of the target, and then paused, gently pulled the trigger, and click .... the firing pin was in. Nothing. "What the hell?" I whispered. Then I counted aloud to thirty, and then slowly opened the bolt and BANG!

Brass and aluminum fragments blasted in all directions. The combination of surprise and shock and blood everywhere and being blind in my right eye was overwhelming, but I knew I had to stop the bleeding and somehow get help. I managed to gather up my shooting blanket and tried to push it against my right eye and jaw. The explosion had blown fragments into my shooting glasses and forced them off of my face, and metal fragments had sliced me, but fortunately they had not embedded, and I was able to hold the blanket there shaking as I struggled with my free hand to get to my cell phone. My left eye was still fine, it wasn't swollen yet, and I was able to call 911. As the operator said, "The ambulance is on its way, hang on," I remember groaning out a "Thank you," and then lying on my wounded side to help relieve the pain while simultaneously applying pressure to the wounds on the shooting side of my face.

I could hear out of my left ear. And as I lay there I was startled by the sound of large shifts and sifts of gravel and small stones grinding behind me. I was weak and going into shock and stiffening up when his massive paw hit my shoulder flipping me onto my back and then swatted my wound as if in slow motion—raking his claws over my forehead and downward just under my eye socket and tearing loose the flesh of my already damaged right cheek. Then a high power rifle boomed and the grizzly stepped over me and blocked out the sun and his shadow passed and he slowly shuffled through the gravel and away until there was silence and then the sirens in the distance wove in. I was soaked in blood. I fought to press the blanket back over my face, and then I heard a dog barking, and then I felt a warm tongue licking my hand as I held the blanket firm, and then I heard heavy human footsteps and a man yell, "Smash your furry ass down! Son of a bitch!" And then the licking stopped and I heard footsteps heavily running over the gravel and then a few distant barks and then gaps in time as if the runner was jumping lightly like a deer as I sank into darkness.

Then I woke up in the hospital. The paramedics had bandaged me and got me to the Prince George emergency room in time. I had lost a lot of blood. My head felt like a swollen rock and I could only see through a slit in my left eye. The doctors had spent over seven hours in surgery stitching up my skull and eye socket and cheek and inserting metal pegs into my damaged jaw bone.

The main surgeon, Dr. Frankincense, explained to me, "That grizzly bear seriously damaged your face,

Thomas, but the good news is that you won't be blind in your right eye. Your eyesight will be fine."

The socket of my right eye was in bad shape thanks to the raking of the bear's claws, but the eyeball itself would be okay. A miracle of sorts with the bear combined with my high quality shooting glasses, saved my vision. The glasses helped when the partially ejected cartridge exploded, and the miraculous helped when the bear tried to rip off my face but my eyeball fit exactly between the spacing of his massive claws.

I remember lying there in the hospital bed and flashing back to when I first took the Canadian Firearm Safety course as a young man and how one of my instructors told us that he once owned a gun shop and had in his front display window a pair of shooting glasses with a razor sharp metal fragment buried in their lens, a vicious barb miraculously held back to the exact distance required to clear the original owner's eyeball.

Dr. Frankincense explained that they did all they could for me in surgery, but unfortunately the appearance of the right side of my face—my shooting side, the side that rests against the gun and looks through the scope—would be significantly disfigured and would remain that way. The positive news was that I would be able to continue shooting. My eyesight would be fine. I asked him if they had taken pictures of me when I first came in and during the surgery, and he said they had—it was standard procedure for health insurance purposes. And when I requested copies, he said there would be no problem. He'd forward them to my email that same afternoon.

As a first-aid attendant, I have always been fascinated by before and after pictures of accidents. Looking at them has always reinforced the obvious importance of my work. In fact, many years ago what really inspired me to become a first-aid attendant was a gruesome 'before' picture juxtaposed with an astonishing 'after' picture in the introduction to my first-aid training course textbook. In the 'before' picture on the left side of the page was a young man's sawed off hand hanging by a few tendons and a remnant of flesh covered in crusty blood, and on the right side of the page was the 'after' picture of that same hand all cleaned up and stitched back together and operating well with only some pale white scars remaining, and the caption beneath the picture described how the fast and efficient first aid this young man received was responsible for him not losing his hand. It was functional and he was fine. I have always remembered those images. They've stayed with me and motivated me.

And so I valued the pictures that were taken immediately in the emergency room by the nurses while the doctors worked on me, and I followed them up with numerous selfies while in the hospital recovering, and especially when the bandages were changed and the scars started to heal, and a few more once the bandages were off for good and I was back at work. I thought it important to document my case fully because it was a catastrophic combination injury—gun accident and bear attack.

I didn't pick up the phone when Johnny called me on Sunday night. I was in no condition to talk, but I did see her missed call and phoned her on Monday from the hospital. I told her that I'd been injured by a bear but that I'd be fine, not to worry, and there was no need to fly out or anything. But I didn't elaborate on how serious the damage to my face was. She had been so happy the last time I heard her voice and I didn't want to upset her. She said she'd be "praying to St. Hubert" for my recovery and asked me to please call her every evening, and I agreed. But I avoided Skype, didn't tell her the full truth, and certainly didn't send photos. I told her I'd be able to return to work in two weeks and I'd be more comfortable just talking on the phone until then, and she agreed that that would be fine.

"As long as you are okay, Tom, I'll go along with whatever you think is best," and I thanked her for her patience.

CHAPTER TWENTY-ONE:

I was stable after two weeks and went back to work on a Monday. All men have scars, some are inside, and some are visible. The injured workers that I treated were strangely impressed that in spite of my facial disfigurement, I wasn't in the slightest deterred in my plans to continue with international shooting as a profession. Their lack of survival instinct seemed strange to me. Anyway, I had to deal with more important matters.

My face was healing well, but the damage was significant and permanent. Dr. Frankincense explained that plastic surgery, given my extreme mutilation, would leave me looking rubbery and fake. He said that was his honest opinion, and with that said, that option dissolved for me.

I really needed to tell Johnny the full truth. I couldn't just leave her in a partial vacuum. I was uncertain about how she would react, but I was hopeful that our relationship was solid enough to handle anything. I had been handsome, according to her, but that was past tense now. I had my collection of photos documenting my injury, and although it might seem gory or weird to anyone outside the medical profession, I decided that it was time to send Johnny the complete collection documenting my horrific entrance into emergency and the stages of my progressive healing.

It was Tuesday night, and I prefaced my email by saying, "Before you open the attached folder of photos, please brace yourself because the first ones look extreme, but the latest ones look much better. I didn't want you to worry before, but now that I am healing and in good health, I want to give you all of the details. Don't worry. The doctors have confirmed that aside from the scarring which will be permanent, my eyesight, nerves, and overall health are fine. It could have been so much worse." "Love, Tom"

Then I hit the send button and waited for Johnny's response. It was just before 8:00 p.m. and usually Johnny was relaxing at home at that time, so I figured she'd either phone immediately or use Skype or email back within an hour or two, but she didn't. So I re-sent the message without the attachment just in case the folder of photos was too large.

I put on a pot of coffee and tried to stay awake all night and wait for Johnny's response, but sleep overwhelmed me and I dreamt that I was buried under a six-foot layer of crushed gravel with a D8T CAT bulldozer in low gear barely moving its massive wait over me. Then I suddenly left my body and found myself floating and looking down and yelling at the machine operator to dig me out, but his diesel engine was too loud and his face was set like blank stone and unaware of my presence either above or below him. Then my dream shifted back to my college years and I was in the library. I was reading Faulkner's *Light in August*. I'd never read him before and I was stunned by his genius. He'd just taken ten pages to allow a mule to walk thirty feet in the stifling heat with the wagon's ungreased wheels mythically turning at an almost undiscernible speed while the mule's ears occasionally twitched and became the highlighted action. The author's outrageous sentences, with their strung modifiers like rag beads on worn ropes, were like nothing I'd ever seen before. Then my dream shifted to the first time I saw Johnny in the Shelby at the car show and I felt her trying to rip the pocket of my Levi shirt. And then my alarm went off and I took a cold shower and dragged myself to work.

When after three days I still hadn't heard back from Johnny, I assumed the worst. I phoned several times on Friday and texted her and emailed her, but all I got back was silence. It seemed clear that she had been overwhelmed by the photos, no doubt depressed by the repugnance of my disfiguration, and she couldn't find the courage to let me know that we were finished as a couple. In the wedding magazines you never see photos of goddesses smiling next to husbands who have been ripped to shreds in the bush. The sick humor of such an advertisement would be nauseating. That's no woman's fantasy. I felt so bad for her. Her ideals were lofty and medieval, as she confessed, and I wanted to release her with love.

And so, to cushion the blow of what I had become and free her from our engagement so we could both get on with our separate lives (what the psychologists nowadays call "healthily uncouple"), I wrote her a long email explaining that I completely understood her dilemma and wasn't in any way judging her. That she now found me repugnant was only natural. I sent it off around 8:00 p.m. on Friday night.

In that email, I confessed, "Johnny, I don't know if it's because I've seen so many guys get their teeth kicked out in fights and men cut up and broken on the job—a psychiatrist would know better than me—but my romantic fantasies and dreams have always been hyper-focused on your physical perfections. Never have I visualized you in a future state where your teeth are broken or your lips are bruised, or you are disfigured in any way. In that sense my love has been shallow. I'm sorry."

I bluntly confessed that from my male perspective I was grateful that my reproductive organs and eyesight were 100%. Those were my top priority.

"Any man who can't get it up, immediately contemplates suicide," I told her truthfully.

But I was good to go as far as survival goes. I told her I loved her and didn't for a second expect her to endure the embarrassment of marrying and then endlessly enduring a disfigured man. I wanted her to be happy. She was released from the engagement. I was okay. I was honestly optimistic, I told her. Some people classify people as glass half full or glass half empty types, but I said I was the kind of person who was grateful that the glass existed at all, that there was no reason why I had come into being in the first place, whatever time I had was a gift and I was happy to have it. I told her I could still shoot. And to help her lighten up and let go, I joked about how in his blues classic "Red House," Jimi Hendrix, when he realizes his lover is out of the picture and he is alone, sings,

"But that's okay, I've still got my guitar," and then rips into a ferocious cosmic solo, and after that, in the final verse sings, "If my baby don't love me, I know her sister will," and then optimistically crashes the final bars of the song down smoothly. I told her that I still had target shooting and fishing, and that these were extreme passions that could be savored as a single man and I could happily grow old and close to nature alone. I'd be fine, and as Austin says to his wild brother Lee in Sam Sheppard's TRUE WEST, "A woman never was the answer." And knowing that she liked old movies, I added how Humphrey Bogart always seemed to be "in a jam with a dame," but he survived, and I would too. I assured her that I actually believed what I was saying. I was not devastated. I understood, and what we had was good while it lasted. Like all beauty in nature, it was destined to fade. That was reality, not romantic fantasy.

It was a long email. And I hoped it would get a response and help us find closure. I didn't mention the possibility of remaining friends because I didn't want that. It would be best to heal and move on alone. But there was no reply that weekend.

On Monday I phoned her and texted her several times from work, but nothing. That night I ate dinner and then showered. And around 9:00 p.m. there was a knock on my trailer door. Through the window I could see that it was Johnny. I opened the door in disbelief. She looked incredibly radiant and natural. She was wearing white runners, faded blue jeans, a simple white T-shirt, no jewelry, no makeup, and her pretty hair was pulled back away from her face by a simple white ribbon at each temple.

Shocked to see her, I said, "Please come in, Johnny. I am sorry about how things have turned out. I've been trying to contact you ... "

But as I spoke she smiled and put her right index finger gently against my lips and held it there as she entered and shut the door behind her and locked it.

"Not a word," she said, still holding her finger on my lips, "Shhh. Where is your bed?"

Obeying, I pointed to the room to the right of me.

As she warmly gazed at me, she slowly made the gentle sound, "Shhhhhhhhh," and steered me backwards into my bedroom and closed the door behind us and sat me down on the edge of the bed and then motioned me to lie flat on my back. Then she whispered firmly, "No talking," and I nodded my silent "yes."

I'd never seen Johnny unable to control herself before. What happened next was private, but I can say that after we finished making love for the third time and we were lying there exhausted in each other's arms steaming with satisfaction on my bed in my trailer, Johnny explained to me that when she was in her late teens, and she was into steelhead fishing but Sally was into hunting, she experienced an epiphany of sorts when Sally suggested that they spend nine days alone in a rented cabin at Barrier Lake. Sally wanted them to pray a novena to St. Hubert, the patron saint of hunters.

"That week we prayed there in solitude," she said as she rested her head on my chest, her silky hair against my skin.

"We hiked along the lake shore and up into the adjacent mountains, and we shared our deepest romantic hopes. And when the sun set each night and darkness moved slowly inwards over the lake, around our campfire we heard crackling in the blackening depths of the forest around us in that grizzly country and we got back into our cabin and Sally kept her rifle close by in case the cabin door crashed down in the night."

She explained how in those late evening hours, in that forest solitude, with the campfire dying out and glowing in the thick dark, Sally had shared a secret fascination.

Sally began with the hunting books that she had absorbed like oxygen during her early teen years, but then moved on to the rugged sexual terrain of her historical pioneer women books, replete with black and white photos of mauled men and extensive letters (never dreamt to be read by anyone except the female confidants they were addressed to, plus several written to the men being pursued, all so-called proprieties thrown to the wind) written by courageous women of the time period who were totally turned on by these wounded and disfigured men. For these women, the facial disfigurations and bodily creases of fibrous healed sinew and masses of scar tissue were macho icons of male fertility. Not all women, certainly not the most delicately domesticated citified ones, liked these men, those women were repelled by their scarred exteriors, but the single frontier women, those who would become the child bearers and house defenders with their .30-30 Winchesters while their husbands were in the fields and bush, for those deep-rooted, vigorous, wilderness women, these mauled men were a pure rush.

An unmarried woman in that frontier culture watching one of these scarred single men chop firewood shirtless and covered in sweat, hacking and swinging, shoulders and limbs sweaty and writhing with claw marks and ridges of scar tissue, and maybe pausing to pant while his strong chest sucked in oxygen to refuel, and panting there with sweaty forearms wiping the drool and sweat from his bitten and torn face, a single woman in that frontier culture would look on a man like that and blush ruggedly at the fact that her underwear was soaking wet, and she'd adjust her full-length dress over her wet inner thighs and pulsate with desire.

Johnny was fascinated. She told me, "There was a deeply erotic, grounded, courageous, sweaty feel to the look of these damaged men. They were the antithesis of the city-boy models with their touched up makeup in the glossy magazines."

And on the last night of their retreat, Johnny had an overwhelming dream: "I saw, as it were from an aerial perspective with their scattered wilderness cabin roofs lifted off, hundreds of young pioneer couples on their wedding nights in candlelit bedrooms shaking the timbers of their cabins as they conceived strong frontier children. And when I suddenly woke up, my nipples were hard and my inner thighs were soaked, and my esthetics of masculinity had been forever transformed."

"That's quite a story," I said as I held Johnny there against my chest with her soft red hair against my skin, both of us satisfied.

"It's all true, Tom. The only problem is you used to look good to me, but now you're simply irresistible." And she smiled widely, relishing her flawlessly integrated Robert Palmer reference.

"We should speed up our wedding plans so I don't have to wear out our local priest's patience in the confessional. Okay? It's not a sin that I can't resist you, it's just awkward that we're not married, and I'll be able to love you with more energy and creativity once we receive the sacrament."

"With more energy and creativity?" I asked in disbelief.

"Oh yeah," she grinned, "We're just getting warmed up, Tom."

"DING!" I said.

CHAPTER TWENTY-TWO:

There would be no more Gold Motel rooms for Johnny now. She was resolved. She had brought two full suitcases to my trailer and she had no intention of sleeping anywhere except in my bed, and so we agreed that we'd get married as soon as possible. As long as Sally and their mom could be there that would be good enough. Johnny was adamant that before we could marry I had to meet her mom Clara in South Bend and get her blessing. So she called her, shared the exciting news, and let her know that I was on my way. My cab would be showing up at her place around 8:00 p.m. on Tuesday night. Johnny would stay behind and make all of the arrangements with Father Lawrence at Sacred Heart Parish, and arrange for Sally to fly out for the wedding on Saturday.

The four-and-a-half-hour Air Canada flight to Illinois was good. As I was boarding, I noticed that the plane's engines bore the silver Rolls Royce insignia (*RR*) and I felt more secure. I also figured, if that baby went down at least we'd go down in style, with flames roaring out of the best engines on Earth. Nothing went wrong. Once we landed, I gave the cab driver the address at the airport. He was an extremely friendly heavyset French Canadian man with a thick accent. He was obsessed with The Fighting Irish and had gone to great lengths to secure a work visa in the U.S. I couldn't get a word in edgewise once I mentioned that I loved football too, but that was fine. Just listening to him was an experience.

I was impressed when we got there. Clara had a large modern apartment at 3999 Rose Crescent, not 300 yards from the southern end zone of Notre Dame Stadium. Being on the twentieth floor, she could actually see most of the field as games were in progress, and the roar of the fans was overwhelming and she loved it. When I pushed the button on her intercom and she said "Hello," I said that it was "Thomas Tems," and she excitedly replied, "Johnny's love! Come right up dear," and buzzed me up.

In the elevator I tried to visualize her, but her image resisted me. It hit me that Johnny had never shown me a picture of her father or mother. I'll never forget the moment she opened her apartment door. She literally was Johnny's identical twin, only twenty-six years older. Her red hair was pulled back in an intellectual bun, and her brilliant emerald eyes radiated through her thick-rimmed scholarly glasses. She looked very fit and was wearing a gold and navy blue Fighting Irish sweatshirt. At first sight my face shocked her, but she seemed to absorb me and love me in a matter of seconds and right away I felt comfortable. By her reaction I assumed that Johnny must have forwarded my file of photos earlier and discussed my circumstances with her before she even showed up at my trailer. Clara warmly smiled, exactly like Johnny, and I could see the genetic reflection. She was very happy to see me and welcomed me in generously.

"It's so wonderful to meet you, Tom. Johnny has been going on and on about you since she first visited the project site at Vermilion Lake. She says you've respected and loved her like a real gentleman, and that means a lot to me. God bless you, Tom."

Clara got us each a cold bottle of mineral water from the fridge.

"She's an incredible young woman, Ms. Nostal. She's easy to love," I said.

"Please call me Clara, Tom. We're almost family now, and it sounds like we will be by Saturday."

"With your blessing we will be married then."

"Please sit down. Let's talk."

The mineral water was so cold and carbonated that I had to drink it in small sips. Clara's apartment was ultra-modern with large windows and clean egg-shell white walls and decorated with thin iron sculptures and large soft-colored abstract paintings, but the east wall of her living room was starkly a wall of contemplation. Centered there was a crucifix about three feet in height. It was cast metal and very dark. The blackish, gunmetal gray figure of Jesus Christ was realistic and it seemed to be engulfed in pain.

"I've never seen anything like it," I said as I gestured towards the sculpture. "The intensity surprised me."

Clara replied, "It's an original work by a Catholic sculptor from Switzerland, a dear friend of mine named Rainer. He gave it to me as a gift before he died. He was so young when he left this world."

Clara sighed and indicated her gratitude by placing her right hand gently against her chest.

On either side of the crucifix were two large paintings of angels, one robed in green, the other in blue. They were original works as well, and executed in the style of Fra Angelico. Clara had bought them from a young woman at the New York Academy of Art. They were graduate students at different schools, but they shared a passion for sacred art and became friends after meeting at a museum one Sunday after Mass at St. Patrick's Cathedral. Clara had a Master's Degree in Counselling Psychology and had been working with severely traumatized youth for the last eleven years.

"Johnny is a very sensitive young woman, Tom. A deeply spiritual woman."

"She is."

"From a little girl, she has been pure of heart. A blossom for God."

"I've seen her love for God. I'm not sure I really understand it yet, but she is a wonder to me, and special beyond words. I've never met another woman like her."

"Do you share her faith, Tom?"

"To be honest, Clara, I can't say that I do right now, but I certainly support her faith, and I've promised to continue to do so if we marry and have children."

"God bless you for that, Tom. She will always need your support. You must always help her to get to Mass every Sunday."

"Sure."

"You must promise me that you will, Tom. Can you with a clear conscience make that promise? You will be sure that she gets to Mass every Sunday?"

Her serious tone surprised me, but her face was kind and full of concern for her daughter and so I said, "Yes, I can. I can and do promise to get Johnny to Mass every Sunday once we are married."

"And you understand what marriage in the Catholic Church means? That it is forever, until death parts you and Johnny? Are you sure that Johnny means that much to you?"

"She is a miracle to me. When I am with her I am happier than I've ever been in my life."

"She is a beautiful woman now, Tom, and physical appearance naturally has a strong hold on a man, but she will grow old and change."

"We both will. Our bodies will age together and we'll be there for each other. Our love won't die. I'm sure of it."

"You are sure?"

"Yes, I am sure."

"You will protect her and always love her, Tom? You are sure of that?"

"Yes, I promise that I will protect her and always love her."

Clara stared firmly into my eyes, as if scanning my inner soul and clicking the pieces of its mechanisms into an evaluative order for final determination, and then something seemed to suddenly relax and gently rotate behind her green eyes and lock into place and she seemed satisfied with my answers and surprised me by suddenly popping in a fresh magazine loaded with shooting questions.

"Johnny tells me you're a shooter—a lover of accurate guns."

"I am. It's my passion."

"Have you ever killed anyone with your guns?"

"I certainly have not," I said, shocked at the suggestion that I was a killer.

She smiled—obviously jesting with me—and said, "But Johnny tells me you hope to make a living with your guns. How will you do that, if not as a hired killer?"

"Actually, I am training to compete at the professional International Level in 1000 meter target shooting with my one and only gun, my Sako TRG 42 .338 Lapua Mag rifle. She's my baby."

Clara's face lit up like a flare, and she joyously exclaimed: "You own and shoot a Sako TRG 42 .338 Lapua Mag rifle?"

"I do, and I passionately reload my own 1000 meter target rounds."

"Let me get this straight. You love shooting long range PLUS you love reloading?"

"I do. Especially with 250 grain .338 Sierra BTHP MatchKing bullets."

"You love Sierra bullets too? This is incredible."

She was happy to the point of trembling and said, "BANG! And I do mean, BANG! You have my blessing, Tom. Listening to you, I hear the voice of my husband Roman. I know he will approve of you."

And then her expression suddenly changed, as if she had let something slip out, or she had triggered a sad memory with her own words.

"He *will* approve of me?" I said puzzled.

It was obvious that Clara was upset and trying to gather herself. After a few seconds her face indicated that her thoughts had clarified and centered and she said, "Yes, Tom, he *will* approve of you. As Catholics we believe in what's called the communion of saints. I don't know if Johnny has explained this to you?"

"She has said a bit about it. They are the people who have died but are really still alive, but in another dimension of sorts."

"That's correct, in the presence of God. Roman is alive in the presence of God, and I believe the Lord will let him see you, and that he will approve of you and pray for you in heaven. Roman was fiercely protective of his daughters, Tom, and he'll want you to be the same way."

I silently absorbed her serious words. This was the climax she had been building towards, and then I made eye contact and held it and promised Clara, "I will be her defender."

Clara was radiant and replied, "Then it's confirmed. You have blessings from both me and Roman. The bride's parents approve of you. I'll see you in Church on Saturday. I'll get all of the details from Johnny. I'll call her as soon as you leave."

I took a cab back to the airport and caught the 11:00 p.m. flight back to Prince George. I had a good, four-and-a-half-hour satisfied sleep on the plane. And once we landed, I wolfed down a large coffee and ham and eggs at the airport and then got into the company pickup and drove back to my trailer.

The road to Vermilion Lake was beautiful in the strengthening morning light. The hills seemed a softer gray and the sky a starker pure blue, thinner, fresher, stretching deeper back and up. I only saw a few vehicles, one large truck and some tourists heavily loaded with camping gear. They were passing through the landscape, like me.

When I got home early Wednesday morning, back to trailer #59, I quietly turned the key in the lock so as to not wake Johnny. For a flash of a second I thought of the countless men on Earth who might fear the possibility of their partners not being alone as they entered unexpectedly as I was entering, and then I thought of Johnny and the fact that I trusted her absolutely, that any scent of infidelity would be repugnant to her, literally poisonous, and I recalled how she thought of herself as a freak, a medieval freak. And I entered silently absolutely certain of her loyalty, and I thought of her love for me and her welcoming of me into her deepest inner life forever and I realized what having the chance to marry her really meant and I felt unbelievably grateful and humbled.

That morning there in the early daylight, with the sun glowing through the curtains, was the second morning in my life that I beheld her in my bed, and she looked even more beautiful than the first morning—delicate and open there with her lovely red hair loose and glossy over our pillows and her arms stretched outwards as if gently claiming rights over the whole of the bed and a faint smile of secure satisfaction still there on her slightly parted lips. She looked like "a blossom for God" there, and more than I could ever express I wanted to love her and honor her and defend her. Looking at Johnny resting there, I silently vowed in my deepest heart to do everything in my power to make her the happiest woman who had ever lived on Earth. I wouldn't hold back a fiber of my being. It all had a medieval feel to it, and I liked it.

CHAPTER TWENTY-THREE:

We were married on Saturday at 1:00 p.m. by Father Lawrence at Sacred Heart church in Prince George. It was basically a private ceremony with no guests or reception. The regular choir sang a few pieces to the best of their ability, but they were nothing you'd record for posterity. Johnny and I wore the same clothes we wore on our first visit to Luigi's House, she in a white dress and me in my sports coat and black jeans. Clara lent us her and Roman's rings until we had time to buy our own in the near future. Sally was dressed in a dark brown dress suit with a white blouse—reflecting the habit of the order she was now a novice in, and her hair was cut very short and brushed back under her black novice's veil. Her intense blue eyes smiled at us as we walked down the aisle after the service was completed, and for a moment she targeted me and approvingly looked through me. I was the complete stranger her sister had fallen in love with, and she approved of me. I was grateful for that closure. And as we walked down the aisle after the service was completed, Clara's intense green eyes gazed into me with loving approval and confirmation of all of my promises. We had a deal.

Then the four of us went to Subway for a late lunch (foot-long meatball marinara subs and large chocolate milks all around) before getting Sally and Clara back to the airport to catch their respective flights: Sally to Montreal and then from there by bus to The Hermitage of St. John of the Cross in Labellecruz where she had entered into the Carmelite novitiate, Clara back to South Bend and her young trauma patients, and Johnny and me back to our new family-size trailer,

trailer #69, one block over from my old trailer #59, and one block closer to the edge of the lake. By wedding magazine and romantic movie standards, I guess you'd have to say that our ceremony was an anticlimax, but our love was real and the sacrament was real. Everything was solid.

In the months that followed our wedding, there were increasingly intense seismic waves associated with our lovemaking in trailer #69. Johnny and I could see it, but of course we kept it secret and did nothing because we were mystified. Circumstances forced us to take action, however, after the night our first child—a daughter—was conceived. That night the seismic waves were so intense that they were no longer waves plural. Together they had fused into a single massive wave, and when Johnny and I furiously reached simultaneous orgasm the earth literally shook and an ancient geological fissure at the bottom of Vermilion Lake spread open and geologists estimated that seven million tons of lava violently erupted skywards in the center of the lake. After the quake had settled and the turbulence cooled and the huge clouds of steam cleared and scientists were able to move in and assess the area, they found that a small island had formed at the center of the lake—exactly at the diagrammed intersection points between Windhover Creek's entrance and exit of Vermilion Lake as Johnny had imagined in her plans—an island like the many little specks of paradise surrounding the main Hawaiian Islands.

As soon as this major event hit the news, the older conservative land investors started a selling frenzy to get rid of their properties at the lake, but the younger risk-taking investors eagerly stepped in and bought every lot they could. They were pumped. Johnny's project had taken on a dimension she never could have predicted. It was obvious that we had to leave the area before something worse happened, for example, a full-blown Mount St. Helens style blast that would annihilate the entire project, so Johnny sold her lot and we relocated to an oceanfront location.

As newlyweds expecting our first child, and with no birth control anywhere on the horizon (and I was fine with that), we reasoned that if the seismic waves indefinitely continued to emanate from our marriage bed, it would be safest to live in a remote location next to the Pacific Ocean where the vastness of that expanse of water would be able to absorb our waves without threat to people or property.

After a lot of research, we decided to move into an isolated older oceanfront home south of the small town of Tofino on the west coast of Vancouver Island. Johnny and I hiked and camped the entire Wild Pacific Trail before we found a garden big enough to plant our Giant Redwood seeds in. The storms and surfing waves and old growth forests and bears and whales, the uncontaminated tidal pools packed with barnacled rocks and sea weeds and onions and colors and countless life forms glowing, swaying, hungry, fluffing their tissues and filaments, burning in their simplicity; the fresh salty air, misty, erratic, moist, sousing our faces—all of it together was good, good soil for tiny massive tree seeds. We sensed home.

When Johnny and I first visited Long Beach, we parked and walked out 100 yards onto the billiard-table low tide sand beach and stood there together looking west over the endless Pacific waves throbbing and shifting and spraying their salty mist into our faces. I remember vividly how we held hands and faced west, our bare feet pressing into the moist fine sand.

I asked Johnny, "Do you think this ecosystem can withstand our intimacy?"

To which she replied, "Based on my seismic calculations factoring area and geological density squared by the number of fixed structures and permanent residences and multiplied by the seasonal fluctuations of tourists exploring both the easily accessible and more isolated hiking regions, my guess is probably yes, we should be able to freely make love without producing seismic waves that would be harmful to the ecosystem as a whole."

Then my outrageously sexy borderline genius wife continued, "Our seismic waves should dissipate and become diffused within seconds given the vastness of the western ocean floor and the ruggedness of the Coastal Mountains. This area, unlike Vermilion Lake, will not act as a volcanic circumference for our passionate simultaneous orgasms."

And then she burst out laughing and kissed me wetly and firmly with gentle biting and I started to respond. And speaking of wood, we then turned landward and saw the strange shore. For thousands of years the ocean winds and storms have pushed against the edge of the coastal forests. Until that first visit to Long Beach, Johnny and I had always looked outwards and westward. Looking eastward now, as far as we could see both up and down the coastline, all of the trees along the edge of the ocean were slanted back at a sixty-nine degree angle, like the freshly combed-back hair of a young auto mechanic who's finished working for the day and with a thick rich lather of industrial soap in the company washroom has washed the grease off of his face and hands before leaving the shop to go home to please his wife.

I remember vividly how we held hands there and faced eastward, our naked feet pressing into the wet sand, and how we absorbed the scene in wild silence with only the waves behind us as our soundtrack, and then we turned to each other, truly happy, and without any prior cue or context or verbal or physical gesture or any other prompt of any kind—simultaneously, literally at the same second, as if the NHRA Christmas Tree lights at our funny car starting lines were identically timed and set—simultaneously we began singing the chorus of Bob Seger's "Against the Wind," and then burst out laughing and kissed.

And then like a singular unconscious cold wave we splashed awake and realized what the song really meant and our faces suddenly became blank.

Surprised, and with a tender sadness, Johnny quoted the line, "The mountains that we moved," and said to me, "That's what you had with Sally, and now have with me," and tears started to form in her green eyes.

And I held her tight and replied, "You're right. With Sally out of my life, for all those years gone, 'I found myself seeking shelter against the wind.'"

Then Johnny said, "Let your heart be at peace, Tom. God has sheltered Sally from the storms and winds. She is safe in the shelter of His right hand."

She continued, "God wants us to be happy, Tom. Lighten up."

And then with a mischievous smirk, she ripped out, "Just because that song is one of the best songs in the history of the world, and just because it reminds us of how as complementary existential entities, male and female, we find ourselves in our postmodern world thrown into being against the ontological horizon of being being being, doesn't mean we can't be thrown towards each other open to new life in the sacrament of matrimony and fall into each other's arms in a sea of troubles and so end them by enjoying the security and ecstasy of extremely frequent simultaneous consummations."

And then she laughed with her unbelievably pretty mouth wide open and her green startling eyes and I held her and kissed her like I always do.

During our research, not just Long Beach, but the whole of the West Coast marine ecosystem blew us away. We decided it would work. As a couple, we have never feared that our seismic waves would reach the pressures of Krakatoa's blast, for example, and so far they haven't. The solitude south of Tofino has been the perfect fit for our lifestyle and circumstances.

I'm keeping my promise to Clara, and every Sunday without fail we attend Mass at the nearby Catholic Church in the Village of Vita Crossing. It's a loving community that accepts me as an interesting-looking respectful observer who doesn't yet receive communion.

We are relieved that during the last two years since we've left Vermilion Lake not even the slightest hint of a tremor has been reported. Here on the West Coast, Johnny considers herself blessed—a fruitful olive vine—and we have a healthy daughter named Chiara. Our second child is growing inside Johnny right now.

Sally has taken her solemn vows at The Hermitage of St. John of the Cross, and she is happy. In a special grotto at the hermitage, they've set up the large statue of Our Lady of Mount Carmel that saved her life during the accident, and Sally prays there daily, for us, and for all people. As planned, Johnny and I have buried Sally's small time capsule in our rose garden facing the ocean.

Mom is meaningfully immersed in her challenging youth work in South Bend and phones us regularly.

Our home is ninety minutes from the Victoria airport, and twelve times a year I fly out for three-day International shoots. I bring home enough money for our family's needs, no luxuries.

Johnny works from home and travels whenever necessary to visit her projects in progress. She puts all of her income aside for the children's education. We have tons of time for each other and our children. We are very happy. And just after we first moved in, a few miles down the coast from us, I got an excellent deal on a good condition 1965 Shelby Mustang that had been parked in an elderly couple's garage for decades. They had almost forgotten it was there. It had belonged to their youngest son who had bought a used Ferrari and left the Shelby behind when he moved out on his own long ago. He had told them that they could do whatever they wanted with the car.

 I am gradually restoring it to mint condition. To the engine, I've added a beautiful Edelbrock intake manifold topped with a Thunder 800 carburetor. And just last week, I had the body painted metallic candy apple red. It turned out great. And once I install the new Thrush Welded exhaust system, she'll be ready for the open road. I keep a thick layer of pink blankets and a few stuffies on the back seat. And whenever the weather is good on Friday nights, once Chiara is asleep, while the withdrawing sun is still warmly hovering at the edge of the ocean, Johnny and I carry her out to the carport and let her dream on the back seat, while in the front we watch and listen to the waves pulsating towards us.

More books from Harvard Square Editions:

People and Peppers, Kelvin Christopher James

Gates of Eden, Charles Degelman

Love's Affliction, Fidelis Mkparu

Transoceanic Lights, S. Li

Close, Erika Raskin

Anomie, Jeff Lockwood

Living Treasures, Yang Huang

Nature's Confession, J.L. Morin

A Face in the Sky, Greg Jenkins

Dark Lady of Hollywood, Diane Haithman

How Fast Can You Run, Harriet Levin Millan

Growing Up White, James P. Stobaugh

The Beard, Alan Swyer

Parallel, Sharon Erby

CPSIA information can be obtained
at www.ICGtesting.com
Printed in the USA
LVHW040346240119
605028LV00001B/34/P